MAID FOR SUMMER

A NOVEL

THE NUBBLE LIGHT SERIES

STACY LEE

WHAT READERS ARE SAYING!

"Maid for Summer is made for me! What a ride. What a read! The characters are interesting and compelling, and the story-line is current and nostalgic all at the same time! Stacy really takes you on a journey with her characters and the tales that never let me down."

- Donna DeLuca Murphy- Reader

"Maid for Summer was a beautiful story of heartbreak and healing, the power of family ties throughout decades, and learning to open up and take chances to love again. Stacy Lee, once again writes a wonderful story I couldn't put down! Highly recommend this book, and reading all the books of the Nubble Light Series. You won't be disappointed!"

-Jennifer DeFeo- Reader

"Stacy does not disappoint. I was captivated from the first word to the last. She brings her characters to life leaving you feeling as though you know them all."

-Mary Jane Quealy- Reader

"Stacy Lee's Nubble Light Series is an accumulation of fictional romance novels that take place at the historical and enchanting Nubble Lighthouse in Cape Neddick Maine... though not imperative, reading the first novels in sequence would greatly enhance the relaxing pleasure of this novel. Watch for book 5 – Maid for Summer. Recommended.

    -READER

"Great read! It had my heart racing at times and tears in my eyes at other times. It had many unexpected moments I wasn't able to see coming!"

    -READER

"I absolutely loved this story. I laughed, I cried, and I wanted more... I was relieved when I finished this book at home because the waterworks hit hard...I didn't find anything I didn't like about this book, besides that it ended...I would recommend keeping tissues nearby for some parts. You won't regret this book. I'd rate it **five out of five stars.**"

    - READER

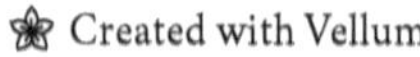 Created with Vellum

For my Parents

I can do it...I can do it...I can do it.

A NOTE TO THE READER

This is the fifth and final book in the Nubble Light series. The books were released in the following order: *The Hundredth Time Around, Future Plans, Never in a Billion, Ten Percent of my Heart,* and *Maid for Summer.*

The Nubble Light series was inspired by my visit to York Beach in 2020. My mother-in-law, Shirley Barbagallo, took my family and me to visit during what ended up being some of the last months of her life. During this visit, we fell in love with the beaches of York, Maine, Cape Neddick, and the Nubble Lighthouse. Because of this, the Nubble Lighthouse holds a special place in my heart.

Also, please be on the lookout for a new series coming soon!

ACKNOWLEDGMENTS

I am truly blessed to be living my dream as a full-time author, and I am overcome with gratitude for the many incredible individuals I have been blessed with along the way. A big thank-you to Lynn and her team at Red Adept Editing. I couldn't do this without you! Also, another huge thank-you to the team at Spark Creative for designing yet another gorgeous cover. Thank you, Kris and the team at the Talking Book. Collaborating with you, Anne-Marie Lewis, and John York on the audiobook production of the Nubble Light series has been truly fantastic. A special thank-you to Allen Redwing and the team at Bookscribs and Story Genius. I can't wait to see the Nubble Light series on the big screen! Thank you to the team at eBook Marketing Solutions. It is truly amazing to see *Future Plans*, *Never in a Billion*, and *Ten Percent of My Heart* hit the Amazon bestseller list! Thank you, Angelina Chrisemer for being the best assistant anyone could ask for.

I could never do this without the love and support of my family! To my husband, Paul Barbagallo, thank you for believing in me, encouraging me, and being my rock. Thank you to my children, Paul and Lucy. I am so proud of both of you and love watching you live your dreams! Paul, you are crushing your first year of high school! We love watching you on the football field, the ski slopes, and the racing track. Lucy, you were a star at iPop! We love watching you perform on stage, whether it is singing, dancing, or acting. And you are doing such an amazing job at track too! Always remember, you are both stronger than you think.

A very special thank-you to my family, friends, and faithful support system. My parents, Karen and Dan DeBruyckere; sister, Kate Giglio, and her husband, Joe; my sister-in-law, Cheri Grassi, and her husband, Mike; my aunt, Pat Fishwick; and my brother, Dan DeBruyckere Jr. Thank you, Kara Holloway and Marisa Berlin for your encouragement and friendship. Thank you, Leigh Anne Hulse and Jessica Delano for always being there. Thank you to my youngest reader, Ella Berlin. You are truly fabulous, and I can't wait to see what the future holds for you! Thank you, Jaclyn Hannan for your constant guidance and support. I wouldn't be where I am today without you! Thank you, Rob Hulse, for everything you have done for my family, for kicking my butt into shape, and for not allowing me to settle for anything less than what I'm truly meant to be.

Thank you to the community of York Beach, Maine, and the Cape Neddick Community. You have been so receptive to the Nubble Light series, and I can't thank you enough for your support. Thank you to Marie and all my friends at Fox's Lobster House in Cape Neddick. A special thank-you to the gift shops in York and Ogunquit, Maine—Whispering Sands, Beach Funatic, the Nubble Lighthouse Giftshop, and the Ogunquit Drug Store.

Of course, I need to thank you, the reader! Thank you for reading my novels and for your feedback. It brings such joy to my heart that you are falling in love with the characters and feel like they are your friends. May you continue to love without hesitation and dream the biggest dreams. Remember, nothing is impossible. You are stronger than you think and there is always a way if you follow your heart. I hope you enjoy book five of the Nubble Light series. Thank you, and God bless!

MAID FOR SUMMER

PROLOGUE

It was the kind of day that even music couldn't make better. Voluminous, plump, heavy tears cascaded from my tired eyes, splashing into my freshly brewed coffee like raindrops in the ocean. Scratch that. Like raindrops in the ocean during a Category 4 hurricane. Or at least, that was how it felt to me.

Have you ever had your heart broken? Have you ever had so much love for a person and so much sadness over what could never be that it overflowed out of your eyeballs like a hailstorm? Every. Salty. Drop. Stings. Did you know that airport tears are a different sort of cry? Did you know that just because you love a person with your whole entire being and even if you would jump in front of a moving freight train for them because you are convinced they are the love of your life, it doesn't mean they'll love you back? If you did know this, would you love them anyway?

I clung to my coffee like a lifeline, but even that had lost its usual magic. The bold, rich flavor that typically warmed my soul was overcome with an intrusive tinge of salt, thanks to the monsoon that was once my face, but I drank it anyway. I drank it because there was nothing else to do. Breathe, I scolded. Inhale—the sweetness of my Starbucks Pike Place blend with the uninviting stench of airport. Exhale. No, really, exhale! More tears. Sobs. Ugly sobs. Awkward side-eye glances. A tissue. A thank-you that was never successfully spoken into existence.

The memory of his words tugged at my heartstrings. Surely they would snap at any given moment, like a guitar string wound too tightly or a rubber band stretched too thin. It's just... It's never going to happen, Summer. I'm sorry. I just... I can't do this.

So let me ask you again. If you survived a broken heart, if you were able to scramble around, picking up the shattered pieces that were once your soul, would you take it all back? Would you erase it all, or would you do it anyway? Love unconditionally, wholeheart-edly, like you have nothing to lose, even though you really have everything to lose.

Please don't ask me to leave. But don't ask me to stay. Leave me somewhere in the middle, where I can pretend my heart's complete.

PART ONE

JULY FIFTEENTH

CHAPTER ONE

JULY 15, 1994

MILLIE BIRD-JENNINGS

The Anderson cottage. In fifty-six years, I had yet to find a place that felt so much like home. A *place*, that was. Did you know that people could feel like home? My husband, Al, was that person for me. Although he was exceptionally busy with our family business, as was I, he still understood the significance of family time, and in that instance, it was my favorite sort of time together—grandparent time.

Al and I had been married thirty-one years this past July. We were blessed with one beautiful daughter whom we named Violet—Vi for short. We raised Violet in York, Maine, where she graduated at the top of her class and earned a full scholarship to Boston College in swimming. It was there she met her husband, Ben, and fell head over heels in love with him. So much so that a slight lapse in judgment on both their parts landed us with the gift of my first granddaughter, Lark, during their senior year of college. Al was furious with Ben, of course. I would never forget the day he yanked the phone off our wall as he paced around the kitchen, hollering,

"Haven't you heard of rubbers, you moron? *This is my daughter's life you've ruined!*"

But Violet was an adult, a very successful adult who'd managed to finish up her last season of swim—along with winning the state championship in freestyle and butterfly—prior to conceiving Lark, so really, what was the big deal? They secured their dream jobs prior to graduating and were married the following year. "All's well that ends well," I always said. Life was too short to get caught up in minor technicalities.

Five years after the birth of Lark, Violet and Ben gave us our second grandchild, Summer Rose. They say there are no two children alike, and this was certainly true of my granddaughters. As I rested on the porch of the Anderson cottage, third floor, rocking in my white wicker chair and overlooking the massive Atlantic with Summer on my lap, inhaling the sweet scent of Johnson & Johnson's shampoo mixed with the ocean air, I said a silent prayer that my twelve-year-old Lark was behaving herself. She started getting into trouble back in the city, where Ben and Violet made a home for themselves. He was an attorney for a major law firm in Boston, and she was a marketing specialist for Converse Shoes. I should probably add that because of this, we would all forever possess highly fashionable footwear. Thank you, Violet.

"Birdie?" Summer asked in a soft whisper. My granddaughters didn't call me Grandma or Granny in a traditional sense but adored Al's nickname for me, "Birdie," deriving from my full name, Millie Bird—now Millie Bird-Jennings—and Summer chose this title for me as well. "Is the tide low, or is the tide tall?"

I ran my fingers through her rich chocolate-brown tresses. "I believe you mean is the tide low, or is the tide high?"

"Yes," she affirmed with a chuckle. "Which one is it?"

I shifted my gaze back to the horizon and over what appeared to be miles and miles of sand with the slightest bit of ocean water at what looked like the edge of the earth. "It's definitely low tide."

Summer nodded, and I pressed my lips to the back of her head, suddenly feeling guilty for correcting her. "It's always good to ask questions," I said. "Never stop asking questions."

"Okay, Birdie," she said, twisting her tiny frame on my lap and curling her knees up under my chest. She snuggled her warm cheek under my chin and pressed her thumb to her lips. I should have scolded her for sucking on her thumb, as this was Violet's biggest pet peeve, but I chose to let it go. Besides, it wouldn't be long before this one didn't want to snuggle anymore either. "I love you, Birdie," she whispered. "I love being here with you."

I smiled and closed my eyes, leaning my head back against the chair, the pace of my rocking increasing, as I was immediately overcome with joy. Summer was such a special child. And I wasn't just saying that because she was my granddaughter, although I knew with every piece of my entire being that I would say it anyway. Summer had recently been diagnosed with a form of selective mutism or SM. Most of the time, she refused to speak. We were unsure at the time of the diagnosis that it was accurate, but it had certainly proven to be true. She would speak to her parents or her sister on occasion but refused to speak at school. The only time she was completely comfortable and willing to speak was at the beach. Specifically, at this beach, at this cottage... to *me*. "I love it here with you, too, Summer Girl."

"I wish everything was this good," she said, suddenly catching me by surprise.

"What do you mean?"

"The beach, the ocean, you… summer. Summer is my favorite season. It's easier than winter, fall, and spring."

"Well…" I started, considering how to answer a question I had often pondered myself. Why was this environment so easy for her? Why were school and the city so overstimulating? Was it the ocean air? Was it my history, *our* history of this beach, this town, and this cottage? Al and I always had every intention of sharing this place with our family, which was why we opened our motel in the first place. "Because," I stated firmly. "You were made for this. You were… you were *made* for summer."

She was quiet for a minute and then asked, "Will you sing me a song?"

"What should *we* sing?" I asked her. I intentionally placed emphasis on *we* because I knew more than anything else how much music helped my granddaughter. I had discovered this early on, and because of this, Violet and Ben had enrolled her in a type of therapy that involved music. "Should we sing 'Somewhere over the Rainbow'?"

"No, thank you," she said politely.

"Then what would you like to sing?" I asked.

"Do you know Guns N' Roses?"

"Guns N' Roses?" I asked, choking back my frustration because in my opinion, a five-year-old little girl should not be requesting Guns N' Roses.

"Yes. 'November Rain' is one of my favorites."

"I don't believe I know that one," I said. "Does Lark listen to Guns N' Roses?" I asked, suddenly curious about her music choice.

"No, it's on the radio," she explained, peeking up at me with her precious smile. "I like 107.3FM and Kiss108 FM. But it's not 108 on the dial, it's 107.9."

"I see."

"Do you know Boyz II Men"

I thought for a moment. The only Boyz II Men song that came to mind was 'I'll Make Love to You,' and that was out of the question for obvious reasons. "I'm sorry, Summer Girl. I just don't think I'm as hip as you are." I kissed her forehead and sighed.

"You're hip, Birdie. What do you listen to on the radio?"

I thought for a moment. "I like the oldies," I admitted.

"You would like Magic 106.7, then," she explained. "What's your favorite oldies song?"

The corner of my lip curled up into a soft smile while the twenty-one-year-old version of my husband flashed through my memories. Those strikingly handsome blue eyes. The way it felt when he picked me up with one graceful sweep away from the rest of the world. "The Flamingos," I said with certainty. "'I Only Have Eyes for You.'"

"Sing that, then," she stated with confidence. "If that song is in your heart, it will come out pretty no matter what," she instructed while sliding her favorite stuffed kitten under her chin.

I began singing, suddenly taken back to that first night on the beach with Al, the cigar smoke and whisky still fresh on his breath as he leaned in and kissed me that first time.

I studied her as her ocean-blue eyes flickered to the rhythm of our tune, surely struggling to fight away sleep. I kissed her forehead and continued singing to Summer, even though she was without a doubt fading into a land of her own dreams. "I only have eyes…"

"For you," she whispered, startling me a bit. I smiled down at her, but my attention shifted quickly at the sound of feet stomping up the steps to the third floor of the Anderson cottage.

"Hi!" Lark shouted, rounding the corner of the porch. Her brunette tresses protruded out of the edge of her head, in what seemed like the world's bounciest side ponytail, her oversized neon T-shirt tied in a knot.

"Hey, girl," I said, placing a finger to my lips as if I was saying *shhh.*

"Sean's coming for lunch," she said, telling me more than asking.

"All right," I said in agreement. "You can make sandwiches. There is bologna and cheese in the fridge. Does Gerry know he's up here?"

As if on cue, fourteen-year-old Sean Anderson jogged up the stairs, his shaggy brown hair bouncing with each movement, and he smiled at me with the same big-hearted grin he presented me with each time I saw him. He might have just been the happiest little boy I'd ever known.

"Hey, Mrs. Jennings!"

"Hi, Sean. Does Grandpa Gerry know you're here?"

Sean wiped sand on the front of his blue jeans. "Yup. I'm supposed to tell you that he wants to have a cigar tonight with Mr. Jennings. And he also told me to bring down some of your famous oatmeal-raisin cookies."

"I'll be sure to let him know about the cigar," I said. "I don't have any cookies freshly made, but you're welcome to the ones that are in the freezer—"

"Then after lunch, I'm supposed to paint the railing," he said, talking at what felt like a million words per minute.

I followed his gaze to the balcony railing, where the paint had chipped over the years.

"That would be lovely," I said. "I'm sure Lark can help you," I suggested.

She rolled her eyes and threw her head back, behavior I anticipated, no doubt.

"Birdie!" she whined. "Sean was going to teach Summer and me how to play his guitar later." She leaned in and lowered her voice so that Sean couldn't hear her. She cupped her hands around my ear and whispered, "Remember, he promised her?"

"How can I forget?" I asked, recalling events from the previous week. "But how else will you earn quarters for the arcade?" I asked with a shrug.

Her eyes lit up, and her side ponytail bounced as she jumped up and down. "Really? The arcade?"

"Really," I affirmed. "After you help Sean paint. And if Sean doesn't teach you how to play the guitar, you know I can show you." I rolled my eyes slightly, thinking of each and every time I'd offered to teach Lark how to play my acoustic.

She threw her arms around my shoulders, almost completely unaware of her sister, who didn't seem bothered in the least by the elbow to her face. "You're the best, Birdie."

"You're the best, baby girl," I said, kissing her on the cheek. "Lark, how is it that Summer knows so much about music? She seems to know of every radio station on the planet."

"Oh," Lark responded with a slight roll of her eyes. "She gets to listen to an FM radio all day at school because she refuses to speak. I tried that once, and I got nothing but a big fat detention."

"Run along," I said with a smile. "The railing isn't going to paint itself."

The slider door slammed behind me as their voices grew softer in the distance. If it was lunchtime already, then Al would be home soon as well. I closed my eyes and took myself back to that night one more time. The poker game had barely been finished for an hour by the time I was in his arms, barefoot on Short Sands Beach, my skirt blowing around me in the breeze. My red lipstick smeared on his white shirt. The back seat of his car as we parked overlooking the Nubble Lighthouse. The shallowness of his breath as he anticipated my kiss. The light in his eyes as they reflected the glow of the moon.

* * *

IN MY OPINION, there were two kinds of people in the world —those who liked to people watch, and those who despised it. I was indeed the people-watching kind of person, as was Al. So, as we sat on my favorite bench outside of the arcade, we did just that. I studied families with small children as they deescalated minor temper tantrums and struggled to remove sand off tiny toes. I observed two teenagers as they slurped melting ice cream cones, most certainly on a first date. I made up stories in my mind about them. How old were they when they met? Were they the loves of each other's lives? Did their parents know what they were up to?

My thoughts were briefly interrupted as I welcomed Al's hand in mine. I leaned my head on his shoulder and closed my eyes. His body was warm and solid and provided the same sense of protection it always had. I clasped my fingers tightly around his and pressed them to my lips for a kiss.

"It's windy today," he said.

"You like the wind," I said, not missing a beat.

"Indeed, I do, Birdie. Indeed, I do."

"Birdie!" I jumped, startled for a beat, and turned my body to the side just in time to see Lark running toward me.

"What is it?" I asked, my concern not going unnoticed.

"It's Summer."

"Well, where is she? Is she all right?" I asked, straining my eyes in the sunlight.

"Can you take her?" she whined.

"Take her?"

"Yes, take her. I almost won the fifteen-hundred-ticket

bonus prize, but she's crying and won't talk to me. Please? Sean is inside, holding my spot."

I nodded in silent understanding. "Well, it sounds like she's overwhelmed, Lark."

"I know, Birdie. It's just… I really want to…" Her voice trailed off.

"I'll go get her," Al said, his tone easy and carefree.

Moments later, Al appeared at the bench, holding Summer by the hand. Summer, red-faced with tears matted through her dark pigtails, gazed up at me with a pout. I extended my arms out to her as she climbed up onto my lap and buried her face into my neck.

"It's too loud in there," she mumbled through her sobs. I placed a gentle hand on her back and began forming small circles with the tips of my fingers along the back of her pink sweatshirt.

"Why do you think I'm out here?" I chuckled. "It's too loud for me too."

"Me three," Al added.

Summer chuckled at this, and the pounding of her heart against my chest began to steady. "You and Papa are funny, Birdie."

"We are funny, aren't we?" I validated, spinning her tiny body around to face the ocean. Rows of seagrass poked up from the sand dune, forming a line roughly six feet from our bench, and just down the hill, the tide was creeping our way, creating what seemed like larger-than-life waves as they crashed on shore. The seagrass swayed from left to right in the breeze, and an even stronger gust of wind took us by surprise.

"It's pretty," Summer whispered to me like she was confessing an important secret.

"The seagrass?"

"Yes, the long tan ones," she affirmed. "It looks like they are dancing."

"It does seem that way, doesn't it?" I agreed.

"They look like weeds to me." Al snorted.

"Do you think they will blow away?"

"No," I said with certainty.

"Definitely not," Al affirmed. "Those aren't going anywhere."

"How do you know?"

I thought about this for a moment. How did I know that these long strands of grassy weeds would not be shaken by heavy gusts of wind that surrounded us? "Because," I started. "Because they are deeply rooted. When something is deeply rooted, it's harder to move."

"So… it's holding on tight?" Summer asked.

"Well, that's one way to think of it," Al said. He tickled the side of her cheek, and she giggled.

I studied him for a moment. His once blond tresses were thinning by the day and shaded with speckles of gray. I adored this look on him. His eyes lit up with his smile as he tickled Summer playfully on her side.

"You're a smart girl, Summer Rose," I agreed. I watched the grass as it "danced" in the breeze as Summer mentioned. I thought for a moment about Summer's comment earlier that morning. *I wish everything could be this easy,* she had said.

"They make it look easy," I said out loud.

"Who makes what look easy?" Al asked.

"The seagrass," I said, gesturing to the blades of grass as they blew in multiple directions. "There are clusters of them. Sixty of them or so? Sticking straight up until the wind comes out of nowhere. They are blown to the left, the right, forward and backward, and all able to stick together as one even though a force greater than them is trying with all its might to separate them."

"Well, now," Al started. "I suppose I never thought about it that way."

"Hang on, seagrass!" Summer cheered from my lap.

"Hang on, seagrass!" Al repeated, chanting as though he was rooting on his favorite baseball team.

I giggled with them, but my eyes were glued to the landscape before me. It was truly amazing that simple weeds blowing in the wind could be so stunning. "How come when I get pulled in what feels like a thousand different directions, I'm not pretty?" I asked Al.

"You're always pretty, Birdie."

"Thank you, dear. But really. They are one big mess, and their mess is a dance. A performance, even. Not knowing when the wind will start blowing and when it will stop."

"Maybe…" Al started, stopped, and started again. "Maybe they can stand strong because they have each other. There is strength in numbers."

I pressed my lips to his cheek and smiled. "They're better together," I affirmed. "Like us."

"Like us," Summer repeated. "I'm going to perform on stage someday," she stated with confidence. "Like the dancing grass."

"You are?" I asked. "Can we come watch?"

"Yes."

"Will you be dancing?" Al asked.

"Singing and dancing."

"How lovely," I said, kissing the top of her head. "Can we have your autograph?"

"What's an autograph?"

"Your signature," Al explained.

"Well, I can't write cursive."

"Don't worry." I giggled. "You'll be able to write cursive by then." We sat together—Al, Summer, and me—studying the grass as it danced in the breeze. And I said a silent prayer for my granddaughter. That someday, she could overcome all her fears. That like those clusters of grass so deeply rooted into the sand, she would overcome her storm, stand firm in what she believed in, and make all her dreams come true. "Come on," I said to Summer.

"Where are we going?" she asked, peering up at me with her sweet blue eyes.

"To the arcade. We are going to be strong, like the dancing grass."

"But it's loud, Birdie."

"Is there a game you like to play?"

"I like Skee-Ball."

"Well, then. Let's go play some Skee-Ball. When it gets too loud, I'll cover your ears."

"Sounds like a plan to me," Al chimed in. "But if you win, I get to pick out the prize," he said with a wink.

"Papa!" she squealed, grabbing our hands and pulling us toward the arcade. "If I win, I get to pick my prize. But if you're lucky, I'll give you one of my Tootsie Rolls."

CHAPTER TWO

JULY 15, 2023

SUMMER ROSE JENNINGS

The Seabird Motel. It was established in 1960 by my grandparents, Millie and Al, and became famous in 1980 when *Yankee Magazine* recognized it as being one of the most prestigious and budget friendly motels on the Maine Coast. The magazine claimed, and I quote, "Enjoy a cup of coffee on the grassy knoll overlooking the enchanting Nubble Lighthouse while indulging in one of Birdie's famous oatmeal-raisin cookies... an absolutely charming establishment."

Yankee Magazine was not wrong. What once started as a charming little bed-and-breakfast has evolved into what seems like an entire estate. The Seabird consists of one main building, two newly remodeled buildings with rooms overlooking the Nubble, the original bed-and-breakfast, an entire building for extended-stay guests, sports and activities clubhouses equipped with an indoor pool and outdoor pool, and a restaurant with both inside and tent seating. The only criticism it receives these days is that its name doesn't do it justice. The community has suggested multiple times that we change the name to something more suitable like the Seabird

Resort and Hotel, for example. My family, however, refuses to change this, as it will forever and always simply be the Seabird Motel, named after my grandmother—Birdie.

Although I was born and raised in Boston, I spent my share of time at the Seabird, it has been years since I have been home. I'm truly grateful to my family for allowing me to set up camp in one of the newest extended-stay rooms. I just wish I were here under different circumstances, that's all. As I settle into the cozy queen bedroom with a sitting area, kitchenette, walls draped in beach tones of blues, grays, so new that the paint still smells wet, I sigh a heavy sigh, secretly cursing the overflowing waterfall of mixed emotions flowing through me. *Yankee Magazine* once declared, "It's cozy. It's breathtaking. It's *home.*" So then why the hell am I not happy to be here?

I shimmy my AirPods inside my ears and select a playlist from Spotify. If I had been prepared for this moment, if I had known this day would come, I would have created a specific playlist. I would have titled it *Back Where I Started... or What in the Actual Hell Happened to My Life?* I would have selected all the best angry-chick breakup music from Alanis Morissette to Taylor Swift's later years, and I would have turned the sound up as high as it could go, put my head down, and pushed through, like many brokenhearted angry chicks have done before me. But as I have recently discovered, you can't plan for life's greatest disappointments. You can't plan for a crisis. You can't predict failure or heartbreak, and lucky for me, I've experienced both in just forty-eight hours' time. So, I select Satellite by Dave Matthews and figure you must start somewhere.

I button the collar of my black polo shirt and tuck it into my khaki pants. I kick my suitcase to the side, making a mental note to unpack at some point. Studying my reflection in the mirror seems to validate that yes, my life is absolutely gone to crap. The last time I wore a Seabird Motel uniform, I was a teenager. Cleaning rooms was my summer gig and then for only a year after high school, and I had been determined to get out of there, on to bigger and better things. And now, here I am, back where I started.

I pull my chocolate-brown hair back and begin braiding it. The thick maroon highlights that I was so excited about just one week ago seem to be taunting and mocking me. "So much for stage hair," I mutter. What had just recently seemed like a fun change for my image out in LA now just seems so... silly. Who needs to look fabulous while cleaning motel rooms? I shrug off my sudden instinct to color my hair something completely different. Ash blond, perhaps? Jet-black? Or even just chop it all off and start fresh, but instead, I tuck a few loose pieces behind my ears and make eye contact with myself. I search my own deep-blue eyes, hopeful for answers or some kind of encouragement, but I fall short. All I discover is disappointment. Disappointment in myself. Sadness. Regret. Heartbreak.

My phone vibrates in my back pocket, and I retrieve it eagerly, hopeful that maybe, just maybe this has all been a dream. I search the screen, eyes wide, fingers unsteady as I swipe open the screen, hopeful to see his name—*Victor*. The mere mention of his name, even just in my mind, sends every drop of blood in my body racing to my head. The warm olive tones of Victor's skin. Victor's dark eyes. Victor's wide, toothy, and sexy smile. Kill. Me. Now. But it's not Victor. I knew it wouldn't be Victor. What are the odds that the man who sends you packing across the country is going to text you less than forty-eight hours later? Probably not great. Instead, my eyes land on a text from my brother, Blake. My baby brother at the ripe young age of twenty-five—he's seven years my junior—has recently taken over the Seabird as manager. And he's taking his new role *seriously* to say the least. Just last week, when I asked him for a place to stay, he told me, "Yes, of course, Summer. That's what extended-stay rooms are for." He even gave me the best pep talk I had received in a long while. Something about knowing I'm not alone because I can count the stars… I don't know. I was intoxicated. *Not* a good moment for me. But then, when I arrived, he handed me my uniform and explained that his top housekeeper had her baby three weeks early and he didn't have time to find a replacement, so, "Tag, moron. You're it."

Blake: Where are you? You haven't clocked in yet.

Summer: Dude. Chill out. I'm on my way. I'm not even unpacked.

Blake: Just… hurry up. I'm putting you in charge of extended-stay today.

Summer: Lucky me.

Blake: Sum, don't make this harder than it needs to be.

Summer: I asked if I could stay in extended stay. Not clean it.

I SIGH and tuck my phone in my back pocket, but it vibrates once more. I pull it out, ready to let my little brother have it, but see Tessa's name pop up on my home screen. Tessa Walker was my college roommate. We lost touch a few years back, as she was busy raising her adopted son, Bex. She now lives in Hawaii with Bex and her fiancé, Desmond. I had been living out in LA when she moved out to Hawaii about a year ago, and since then, we've been talking nonstop.

Tessa: Did you get settled in okay?

Summer: If by settling in you mean I showered and brushed my teeth, then yes. I've settled in nicely. Haven't unpacked a thing. Running to work.

Tessa: Keep your head up. This is just a bump in the road.

Summer: Thanks. It feels more like a sinkhole.

I retrieve my room key and jam it into my free pocket and slide on my sneakers, but I can't leave just yet. Perched over in the corner of my room between my bed and the wall is my guitar case. I sigh, make my way over to it, and have it unpacked in no time. I remove the AirPods from my ears and tuck them away. I pull the guitar from the case and am immediately overcome with a sense of nostalgia from the aroma of wood, metal, and strings. I run my fingers over the body of the guitar, and before I realize it, I'm hugging it like one might hold a favorite stuffed animal or long-lost love. "Hello, friend," I whisper to it in the silence of my empty room. I close my eyes as memories zip through my brain like a flashback in movies. My fingers sliding effortlessly over the guitar strings, my feet tapping to the beat, song lyrics—*my* song lyrics—busting out of me like my life depends on it. The cheering of the crowd.

I rest my guitar gently on the white bedspread. "Just a bump in the road," I repeat to myself. I leave my room and start to close the door behind me. "Just a *little* bump in the road," I say again.

"What's a bump in the road?"

I jump back, almost closing my finger in the door. Apparently, I have a neighbor, and he has overhead me talking to myself. "Nothing," I say, turning in the opposite direction from him, but I pause for a beat, feeling like I should explain myself. This is, after all, the extended-stay building, which means this person is not going anywhere anytime soon. "I was just giving myself a little pep talk. That's all."

This person, my neighbor, is sloping over the porch railing, perched on his elbows, and hasn't taken his eyes off the horizon. I wonder if he's staring out at the Nubble or if he's lost in his own thoughts—or maybe both? His hair is dark with traces of what look to be faded-blond highlights, and it's shaggy, and I can't tell if he needs a haircut or if this is a look he is going for on purpose. He's tall, and when he turns his gaze in my direction, I can't help but notice that his dark eyes seem sad. Then I wonder if I notice this because I, too, am sad. And this makes me sadder.

"Nothing wrong with a good pep talk," he says. His voice is gravelly, and he strikes me as a person who chooses his words carefully and intentionally. I can tell, based on the seriousness of his tone, that his life must not be sunshine and rainbows either. I suddenly feel guilty for judging him, but then, as he looks back in the distance, I realize that I'm not judging, just noticing.

"Do you need one?" I ask, surprising myself with my boldness.

"I don't smoke."

I laugh, louder than I mean to, and I suddenly feel embarrassed. "No," I say, moving closer to him and resting my clasped hands on the railing. I feel my phone vibrate in my back pocket, and I know it's Blake wondering where I am. "I wasn't offering you a cigarette," I explain. "I don't smoke either."

He looks down at me, and I realize that the top of my head barely reaches his shoulder. "Oh," he says, studying me intently. The heat from his stare catches me off guard.

"Oh," I repeat back to him. "I was asking if you need a pep talk."

"A pep talk?" he asks, one side of his lip curling up in a half smile.

"Yeah," I say. "Like, words of encouragement—"

"I know what a pep talk is."

"Oh, okay, then. Let me know if you change your mind. I'm Summer. Summer Jennings."

"Jennings? Like the famous Millie and Al Jennings? And the manager, Blake Jennings?"

"That's me." I sigh, allowing his words to wash over me, validating that I am indeed back home, and I have very much hit rock bottom.

"Blake's sister?" he asks, studying me carefully.

My breath catches in my throat, and I wonder to myself if another human's eyes can light you on fire, because if they can, I might spontaneously combust.

"In the flesh."

"I didn't realize Blake has a sister," he admits.

"He has two. My older sister, Lark, is stationed out in Clearwater, Florida. She's an intelligence analyst for the United States Coast Guard."

"Wow, that's something," he says, nodding his head in approval.

"Yeah, she's *something*," I say, kind of sarcastic, kind of not. My phone buzzes again, and I retrieve it from my pocket, confirming my earlier thoughts that Blake is in fact ready to kill me. "Speaking of Blake, I've got to go before he burns me alive."

"Is that what you do for a living? Clean motel rooms?"

I sigh and pull my braid over my shoulder, grazing the ends with my fingers. A tiny tear seeps out the corner of my eye, and I quickly wipe it. "It is *now*," I admit, choking a bit on my words. I turn away from him in an effort to remove myself from this suddenly uncomfortable situation. Two weeks ago, my ego would have taken a hit. Usually, people have at least heard of me from my time on *Rise 2 Fame*. If I wasn't recognized for winning the nationwide talent show, then I would have been spotted because of my time opening for Katy Perry on tour last year. And if I wasn't recognized for that, surely this stranger would know me from the tabloids, thanks to the negative press I have received over the past week.

"River," he says, his raspy voice interrupting my sadness, if only for a brief second. His tone is so rough and unique it sounds as though it might be echoing through a cave or tunnel. He holds his hand out for a handshake, and I accept it in my own.

"Hi," I say. I silently need to know everything about River. Maybe if I completely fixate on my new neighbor, then I can take my mind off my own misery. He looks to be about my age or even a bit older. Maybe midthirties? Why would someone like him be living at a motel? Why are his eyes so sad? What would he look like naked? I shake my head and wipe the beads of sweat from my forehead. *Get it together, Summer.* "That's a good name, River."

"My friends call me Riv, for short."

"Well, Riv," I say, "it's off to work." My words come out jumbled and rushed. "Let me know if you need anything," I say a bit awkwardly. "You can, you know, put the service sign on your door so I don't interrupt…" My voice trails off, and I wave goodbye, like a child waving to a parent as they leave for school. I silently scold myself for my lack of social skills in this moment.

"Summer?"

I turn so quickly that my braid whips me in the eye. I rub it with my shaky fingers, and I squint to see him through the sunlight. I study him as he leans over the porch railing, his expression serious, like he's about to offer me the solution to all life's greatest problems… or invite me to dinner. I exhale, realizing just now that I was holding my breath. "Yeah?"

"Those little shampoos and conditioners. I could use a few of those."

CHAPTER THREE

JULY 15, 2023

RIVER FROST

*S*he's prettier than I expected her to be—Summer. I mean, I've seen her pictures on social media, in magazines, and on TV. But I guess people always look different in real life, right? I mean, I'm in the movie business. I should probably have figured that out by now. She's way shorter and skinnier than I had expected, and I must admit, she's way prettier without makeup.

I knew she was going to be staying at the Seabird, but I suppose I hadn't expected her to be staying right next door. Blake mentioned she was coming home to work for the motel, but I hadn't realized it would be so soon. She had been out in LA for years, and even though her life was completely blown up only two days prior, I figured she would at least have to pack up her house prior to coming home.

I pull into the parking lot of the movie set and glance at the clock on my dashboard. I have twenty minutes to spare, so I quickly open my Instagram and flip to Summer's fan page. So far, there are no updates on what went down out there, only photos of her last tour and highlights from her time on *Rise 2 Fame*. I check TikTok and Facebook only to find the same. It isn't until I open my Twitter account that I find that her adoring fans seem to have turned on her. I scroll through her Twitter feed to find comments like #scandal, #homewrecker, #phony, and #loser, to name a few. I sigh and run my fingers through my hair, wondering if what Blake said was true and deciding that if so, Summer is going to need a friend to help her through this.

I gather two trays of iced coffees and close my car door behind me. I enter the ten-thousand-square-foot warehouse that we're currently using for the movie set of *The Hundredth Time Around*, a major motion picture based on a book series by a local author. I've been screenwriting for over a decade, and this dude Sean Anderson scored a major movie deal on his first try. Don't get me wrong. I'm happy for Sean. I will just be happier for myself when I finally catch a break. After completing film school out in LA, I made it my goal to start writing scripts and eventually make my way to assistant director or director on a set like this. But plans changed—for several reasons. And now, I find myself on the East Coast in Portsmouth, New Hampshire, working as a production assistant for a movie that Sean Anderson landed on his *first* try. Although, I must hand it to him. I read the book in preparation for my interview, and it isn't bad.

"Morning, Riv," Sandra, one of the other PAs, says as I enter the building.

"What's up?" I say as I begin handing out iced drinks to the appropriate people.

"Thank you," they say one at a time as I finish my coffee delivery and start my necessary PA duties.

I walk through the building that had once been empty, a gloomy, musty structure with a creepy basement vibe, and it has now been transformed into what feels like another world. The energy from the cast and crew alone provides me with more energy than any cup of coffee could. There is a unique energy in the air that comes from the positive collaboration and collective effort.

"Morning," I say to a coworker as I pass through various set designs—a mahogany bar, equipped with a piano, and the second-floor living room and kitchen of the Anderson cottage, complete with a brown-and-tan armchair that belonged to Gerry Anderson. I continue through the set until I come across Sean Anderson's bedroom and Gwendoline's bedroom, designed to look like a cottage bedroom from 1945. Being on set is a feeling I wouldn't trade for anything.

"Big day today," I say to Julia, handing her a call sheet.

"It is," she says with a smile, brushing a bouncy red curl away from her eye. "Today is the day I cheat on Gerry with Joey Chase." She winks and struts away, and I can't help but chuckle.

"Hot brick?"

I turn to see the assistant director, Crawford, holding out his hand. "Sure thing, boss," I reply, taking his walkie-talkie from him and replacing the battery. "Need anything else?"

"As much as I hate to say this, I need eyes on Lawson. We've been looking for him again."

"Sure he isn't a 10:1?"

"The bathroom? If he's been in the bathroom for an hour, then that's a completely different issue."

"Copy that."

I pull my walkie out of my pocket and ask, "Eyes on Lawson?" I shake my head and begin my search for celebrity Lawson Remington, cursing spoiled famous actors everywhere and swearing that somehow, someday, my job on set will move past coffee runs and celebrity stakeouts.

CHAPTER FOUR

JULY 15, 2023

SUMMER ROSE JENNINGS

*D*id you know that the human brain processes the pain of rejection the same way it handles physical pain? So basically, being left out on the playground can feel the same to a child as a broken arm. This must be why people refer to being brokenhearted in the way they do—because rejection *hurts.*

So, when the love of my life, my best friend, told me, *It's never going to happen Summer, you and me. It will never happen.* My brain must have been so confused that it malfunctioned. The rejection I experienced and the pain I endured could have been processed as an actual injury—or worse than that, actually—because we've gone and added insult to injury. Because let's face it, rejection is insulting.

Lark and I took Blake ice skating at the local hockey rink once when he was fifteen years old. He slipped and face-planted on the ice. The deep-red blood trickled out one nostril, and tears leaked out his eyes. Lark asked him what the pain scale was, and he said, "I'm fine, but my pride is bruised. I'd give the bruising of my ego a ten out of ten."

I think that's real. We get rejected, and we get hurt. We

grieve, and we mourn. I guess the question there lies in what do we do next? Do we wallow and accept it, or do we move on? Do we allow it to crush us, change us, and inevitably ruin us, or do we brush ourselves off and get back up again? When is it time to heal? I would never let a broken arm define me, so then why am I letting this? I'll tell you why. Because a broken bone is a setback that we have been taught to manage. We are told specifically that this is the problem and this is how to fix said problem. But rejection? It's invisible. Impossible to cope with when we are in the thick of it. We end up hating ourselves for it, and this leads to even more setbacks if we allow it to define us.

How do I move on from this? Where are the X-rays, the casts, the diagnosis, surgery, physical therapy, lollipop from the doctor, doctor's note to miss work? *Anything?* Where is the medicine to take away the pain? I think the answer is time. Time heals all things, right? Even the worst kind of pain? That's why a sprain is worse than a break. Because a broken bone can heal faster than the tendons, ligaments, and muscles that are damaged in a sprain. So, if that's the case, why don't we say, *my heart's been sprained or torn* instead of *broken?* Because for the foreseeable future, healing seems unlikely.

"Hi, um… Excuse me. Miss?"

I leap into the air, my thoughts shattering around me. I trip over my own foot and land on the hotel-room carpet with a thud. Clearly, I was so lost in my thoughts that I failed to realize the guest in room 709 was trying to get my attention. And apparently, I've been crying. "I-I'm so sorry. I didn't hear you come in," I say, tripping over my words and wiping my eyes with the back of my hand.

"Sorry to startle you," says the quiet, soft voice of a woman standing in the doorway of her room.

"I'm just finishing up," I say, picking my sorry self up from the ground. I wipe my tears on my pants and pick up a dirty towel from underneath the bed. "Thanks," I say, gathering my cleaning supplies and pulling my cart toward me. "Have a great—"

"Oh my God," she squeals. "Aren't you Summer Jennings?"

Freaking A. There was a time in my life I would have enjoyed being spotted for my celebrity status. This is *not* that time. It is only now that I make eye contact with the woman in the doorway. She is roughly my age and has a little blond toddler on her hip. I look from the adorable pigtailed babe to the woman and begin wheeling my cart over the threshold, suddenly needing to escape this situation more than I need air. "Me?" I mumble. "Summer Jennings? Sorry, I think you've got the wrong person."

"Wow! You have a twin, then! What's the word? Doppelganger?"

"Yeah," I say, waving goodbye and keeping my head down. "Pretty cool! I'll have to look her up."

"No, wait!" she shrieks in a tone that is way too happy for how I'm feeling in this moment. "Look. I have her picture right here." She rummages through her beach bag with her free hand.

Oh God, no, I think to myself. I knew there would be more backlash in the media. I'd done everything in my power to avoid it. But sure enough, bam. There it is—Victor and I plastered across the cover of the cheesiest tabloid in the nation. My hands on either side of his face and my lips smooshed against his. My long, dark, maroon-highlighted tresses falling effortlessly over my side profile. The headline: *Shock and Awe! Summer Jennings and Manager Victor Diaz Caught in the Act!* I gulp. *Breathe, Summer!* I silently scold. I inhale deeply and place a shaky hand on my hip. How in the actual hell did they manage to get that photo, in that moment, so quickly? "Wow, you're right. She could... she could be my twin for sure," I mutter, tiny beads of sweat trickling down my lower back.

"The resemblance is truly uncanny. You even have her highlights," she challenges, adjusting her daughter on her hip.

"Mama, beach!" the little girl whines, tugging at the ends of her mother's blond ponytail.

"No baby, no beach. *Nap*," she says, gesturing to a beige pack 'n play nuzzled between the bed and the wall.

"No nap!" she whines, pulling at the strap of her mother's black bikini top.

"It's truly a coincidence," I say, trying with all my might to steady my voice. "Would you mind if I borrow that?" I ask, turning my gaze toward the magazine.

The woman takes a step closer to me, holding it out. "It's really a shame," she says with a sigh.

"What's a shame?" I ask, taking it from her eagerly.

"The artist." She sighs. "Summer Jennings. She was sleeping with her manager, Victor Diaz. *The* Victor Diaz. And considering the circumstances, it's looking more and more like a scandal."

"Well, you know what they say about trusting the media," I say, the shakiness in my voice growing stronger by the second. I can't take my eyes off the photograph, no matter how hard I try. The familiarity of Victor's dark hair, the rigidness of his cheekbones. I remember how he smelled in that moment—a combination of sandalwood and spices, creating an aura of confidence and charm about him. I remember as clear as day how soft his lips felt against mine. His charismatic smile and the glimmer in his eyes when I said something funny. Why is the universe so unfair? My knees grow weak, and I shake the memory away as best I can. "I'll bring it back when I'm done reading it," I say. "If that's okay."

"Of course it is," she says with a smile. "We aren't going

anywhere anytime soon. My husband is working on the movie set for at least the next two months."

"Movie set?"

"Yes, it's going to be a major motion picture. He's the director."

"They're filming here, in York?"

"Yes. Well, most of the filming is taking place at a warehouse in Portsmouth, New Hampshire. But yes, Long Sands, Short Sands, and the Nubble Lighthouse are some of the major filming locations, so Oakley and I get to spend the summer together, beaching it in New England. Don't we, Oakley?" she asks her daughter.

"Oakley," I repeat. "What a beautiful name."

"Thanks," she says, smiling and bouncing the baby on her hip.

"How old is she?"

"She just turned eighteen months," she says with a smile. "It sure does go by fast."

"So they say…" My voice trails off, and I fiddle with my braid. "I didn't realize they were filming a movie in our area," I say, tucking the magazine under my arm.

"It's based on a book. A local writer, Sean Anderson, wrote four books in a series called the Stories of the Nubble Light. I'm sure you've heard of them?"

I think for a moment. Sean Anderson was a family friend growing up, and I hadn't realized he had written a book, let alone a book worthy of a movie.

"No, I… I've been a little distracted," I say, a wave of uneasiness washing over me and suddenly wanting to spill my guts to this stranger.

"You should read them for sure," she says, her voice increasing in speed. "They have them down at the gift shops," she says, motioning over my shoulder. "You will never believe who they cast as the lead role!"

"Who?" I ask, my tone matching the excitement in hers.

"Lawson Remington!" she shrieks.

My jaw all but hits the floor, and my knees grow weak. For the first time in two weeks, I am thinking of something other than the destruction of my career, shattered dreams, and my broken heart. "Lawson. Freaking. Remington?"

"Yes! I got to meet him yesterday. He's so hot and super nice. He's staying over at the Anderson cottage during the filming. He's playing Sean in the movie, and he needs to be at the cottage so he can fully get into character."

"He's playing Sean?"

"Yes. Sean wrote his first book about an experience he had with his wife, Cassidy. So yes, he's the main character, and *Lawson Remington* is playing him!"

"For real?" I repeat, my own voice changing in tone. "He's been my favorite actor since as long as I can remember. My room used to be wallpapered with his posters. I'm pretty sure I had his face on my pillowcase when I was ten."

"Girl!" she hollers. "How did you not know this?"

"I've had a few things going on," I say, my eyes shifting to the floor.

"We should have coffee," she says, telling me more than asking. "I could use some girl talk—no offense, Oakley—and you strike me as someone who could probably use a friend too."

I peel my eyes off the floor and finally meet her gaze. "I—"

"It's okay, Summer," she says with a smile. "I won't blow your cover, I swear. But at some point, I do want an autograph… and maybe a selfie."

I laugh nervously and bite my lower lip. "Of course," I say. "And maybe we can do drinks. You know, if your husband can watch Oakley. I'm suddenly finding it very important that you know what really happened to me out in LA."

"Absolutely!" she exclaims. "How's tonight? I have absolutely nothing going on, and Brad, my husband, has an early night tonight."

"Perfect," I say, regretting the words as soon as they leave my lips. The idea of cleaning up and getting dressed to go out suddenly feels overly exhausting. But the idea of clearing my name, even with just one person, sounds worth it. "Seven o'clock?" I ask. "Sea-Pub?"

"I'll be there," she says with a smile.

"I didn't get your name," I say, a bit embarrassed by this.

"I'm Athena," she says. "But my friends call me Thena."

"It's nice to meet you, Thena. I'm Summer," I say, blushing a bit.

"*Yeah*, you are," she says with a smirk. "But I won't tell anyone." She winks.

"It's okay." I sigh. "I can't hide forever."

"Nor should you have to."

"Thanks," I say. "See you tonight." Then I say, "Goodbye, Oakley!" in my best baby-talk voice. I turn away from them, the slightest bit of excitement flowing through my veins. Drinks with Thena will be a good thing, as I could really use a friend. But first, there's a magazine article that needs my attention, and I can't get back to my room fast enough.

CHAPTER FIVE

JULY 15, 2023

RIVER FROST

I had been searching for Lawson for just about half an hour when the dude finally answered my text.

Lawson: Sorry, man, I slept in. Can you come get me? Scarlett left without me.

River: Dude, you were with Scarlett?

I HAD RESISTED the urge to throw my phone against the concrete floor. Scarlett is the actress playing the role of Cassidy Quinn, and it struck a nerve to hear that the two of them spent the night together. Not only have I always had a secret celebrity crush on her, but she also only recently turned twenty-one years old, and Lawson is approaching forty. Knowing what I know about Hollywood, this kind of age difference shouldn't surprise me, but still, I couldn't resist the sudden urge to tell Lawson Remington to get his own damn ride and call it a day. But I did, however, like my job enough to bite the bullet and go get him. I suppose I could have called him an Uber, but at this point, I consider him to be too much of a flight risk to trust a rideshare.

It had taken me a little less than twenty minutes to drive from the movie set to the Anderson cottage on Long Sands Beach in York, Maine. Lawson had insisted that he stay at the Anderson cottage during the filming of *The Hundredth Time Around,* as he needed to immerse himself in the life of Sean Anderson for his performance to be authentic. Producers allowed this to happen but added a nondisclosure clause to our contracts, preventing us from sharing this information with anyone else, which is also a good reason for me to pick up Lawson instead of sending a stranger to do so.

Now, as I climb the steps of the Anderson cottage to the third floor and knock on the sliding door, I pause to catch my breath, taking in the serenity of the salt air, allowing it to calm my irritability from my toes to my soul.

I breathe a sigh of relief as Lawson appears at the door, pulling his arms into a black leather jacket and kicking on an overly large pair of Dolce & Gabbana sunglasses over his baby blues. "Sup, man," he says, looking more like a college kid in his twenties than a forty-year-old grown man. He runs a hand through his shaggy brunette hair and murmurs, "Sean, Sean Anderson," and holds his hand out for what I imagine to be a handshake.

"Let's get moving, Sean Anderson," I say, turning from the door and heading down the stairs.

"I've been working on that all morning," he calls from behind.

"Crushing it," I say before getting back into my car and starting the engine.

"Sean, Sean Anderson," he says again. This time, his voice is deeper. I ignore him and put my car in drive. Lawson is quiet for a moment, looking out the window as we pass by tourists and beachgoers. "Thanks for coming to get me," he says, his tone sincere.

"Anytime."

"I know how it looks, man."

"How what looks?"

"Scarlett."

"Not sure I know what you mean."

"Come on. The judgment is obvious," he says, pulling his sunglasses down from his eyes and peering at me.

"Well, yeah. I mean, you could be her father, but who am I to judge?"

"Dude, that's just gross."

"But it's true."

"I was just getting into character. We weren't Lawson and Scarlet. We were Sean and Cassidy back in 2001."

"Still gross."

"She didn't think so. You should have seen—"

"Dude, enough."

"Sorry."

CHAPTER SIX

JULY 15, 2023

SUMMER ROSE JENNINGS

The Sea-Pub Restaurant and Bar is a favorite for locals, tourists, and guests of the Seabird Motel and has been for generations. What began as a tiny breakfast joint in the '60s has transformed into a popular dining spot and even a weekend hangout for teenagers and young adults. It's located across the street from the motel and offers seating both indoors and outdoors, overlooking Long Sands Beach. At night when the sun is setting, it is exceptionally beautiful, with the Nubble Lighthouse appearing to be a miniature sculpture in the distance.

I check the time on my cell phone, which reads 7:23 p.m., and for a moment, I wonder if Thena has stood me up. The concerned side glances of the bartender state that he, too, is wondering if I will be flying solo this evening. I was perched on a barstool, sipping water, when he asked me what I wanted to drink. I had hesitated, not knowing if I should wait for Thena or order something prior to her arrival. I decided on water but am currently regretting my decision. My phone vibrates, and I turn my attention to my texts. It's a text from my sister, Lark.

Lark: Hey, Little Twerp. Just checking in. How are you doing?

Summer: Hi. I'm working for our brother and cleaning toilets. How would you be doing?

Lark: He's not so bad.

Summer: Oh yeah? Want to join me?

Lark: Over my dead body.

Summer: LOL. See… it's bad. How are the snowbirds?

Lark: Mom and Dad are good. They are getting settled in at their summer place. They are worried about you, though.

Summer: Do me a favor and keep them away from the tabloids.

Lark: TOO LATE!

"Are you sure you don't want to look at a menu?" the bartender asks.

I glance up at him from my phone. He's cute in a clean-cut, freshly shaven, boy-band sort of way. "Sure, thank you," I say, rummaging through my bag, not even sure of what I'm looking for. I pause like the wind has been knocked out of me when my fingers feel Thena's magazine from earlier. The magazine that I have failed to even open let alone read.

The bartender passes me a menu, and I begin scanning it over, stopping short when I come across the margarita list. Why is it when your heart gets broken that the tiniest things can set you off? One minute, you're fine. You're sitting at the bar of your family's motel, getting ready to have drinks with a new friend, when *bam. Tequila.* And tequila can't just be tequila. Tequila equals Victor, and Victor equals sadness, regret, and an overwhelming ache in the depths of your soul. And you go from being completely fine and considering a margarita to remembering all the tequila you drank with Victor. And then you think about the kiss, the only kiss you ever shared with Victor, and you can taste the sweetness of the agave and the salt that once rimmed his glass and how it surrounded his lips, and you can't help but wonder if that moment, the moment that changed your life, could have been ruined because of too many margaritas.

"Anything stand out?" he asks, wiping down the bar's counter with a towel.

"Excuse me?" I ask, my voice sounding like I'm in a daze.

"Anything to eat or drink?"

I sigh and scan the menu. Tequila. I really want tequila. But tequila has somehow becomes Victor. "I'll have a glass of the Caymus cabernet," I say, my words catching in the back of my throat.

"Coming right up," he says.

I wipe the corners of my eyes with my blouse sleeve and sigh. I wonder if a person has ever been hurt so badly that the tears never stopped. I consider searching Google for evidence of such a thing but decide against it. Instead, I reach in my bag and begin to text Lark back, but my phone buzzes again, and Tessa's name appears on my screen.

Tessa: What's on your playlist? 🎵

Summer: Dan & Shay

Tessa: Song?

Summer: Tequila

Tessa: Damn

Summer: Yup

Tessa: Could be worse, right? Call me if it gets worse. 💜

One of the things I love about Tessa is that she's a therapist. Which means she has been professionally trained in how to deal with a crisis, and that currently makes her my lifeline. On top of her professional qualifications to help me through this mess, she has also gotten to know me well. Well, enough to know that just by asking me what's on my playlist, she can tell how I'm doing. This little game we play has been such a relief for more reasons than one. First, I would much rather talk music than explain my emotions, and if one more person asks me if I'm okay, I may scream.

I contemplate telling her that I'm sitting at a bar alone, but just as I start to text, I feel the distinct feeling of someone hovering over my shoulder.

"What's up, Riv?" the bartender asks, staring through me. "Back again so soon?"

I turn on my stool to see River, my neighbor, passing his debit card over my shoulder with a smile. He seems different to me for some reason, and I'm not sure whether it's because he's traded the outfit he was previously wearing for baggy gray sweatpants and a black hoodie.

"Yes," he says. "I'm picking up the order under Frost."

"River Frost?" I ask. "I bet the kids at school had fun with that one."

"Hello, Summer Jennings," he says with a smile, obviously ignoring me. "Come here often?"

"Is that what you say to all the ladies?"

"Only the *really* pretty ones," he says, his tone overly flirty but his face remaining serious.

"Got it," I say, feeling the heat rise from my neck to my cheeks.

"Here you go, man," the bartender says, handing him a large paper bag.

"Have yourself a good night," River says, nodding in my direction and exiting the restaurant.

I try not to stare at him, but he gives off such a mysterious Tom Hardy sort of vibe that it distracts me from my misery for a millisecond. I reach for my phone, suddenly eager to tell Tessa that the song on my playlist has suddenly changed from Dan & Shay's "Tequila" to "River" by Bishop Briggs, but I'm interrupted when a tall, frazzled blond woman comes crashing down on the barstool next to me —Thena.

"I'm so sorry!" she exclaims. "I totally should have taken your number. My husband ran late on set, and Oakley's stomach is upset. I think she drank the salt water by mistake…"

Her voice trails off as I attempt to get a word in but come up short. Her golden hair is pulled up into a messy bun, and patches of red form on her pale skin, evidence of a day spent at the beach, or maybe flushed from rushing. I can't tell which. Her eyebrows rise up, and her facial expression is animated as she lists reason after reason for her tardiness.

"Thena," I say, holding up my hand. "It's totally fine. I haven't been here long, I swear."

The bartender sets my glass of wine in front of me and greets her.

"Really?" she asks, looking from myself to the bartender as if needing a second opinion.

"Really," I say. I hand her a menu and sip my wine.

"Take your time," the bartender says.

"Oh, I don't even need the menu," she says with a chuckle. "It's a no-brainer for me."

"Okay, then. What can I get for you?" he asks.

"A blueberry margarita," she says, clapping her hands like

a child ordering her favorite ice cream. "They are to *die* for. Salted rim, please."

Just a little over an hour later, Thena has managed to put back two blueberry margaritas, and I have allowed the bartender to convince me that purchasing the bottle of Caymus would be my most cost-efficient option. We have devoured a basket of fried clams and pub fries, and I have strategically avoided Thena's multiple questions regarding LA, as I wasn't entirely ready to answer them. Instead, I redirected her questions back at her, and I learned quickly that she enjoys talking about herself, her family, and her daughter.

Thena met her husband in her hometown of Anaheim, California, during her sophomore year of high school. She spent most of her time after school in the library, as she wasn't very involved in sports or clubs. Instead, she caught up on homework after school and served as a tutor for struggling students. Her husband was among those struggling in Algebra II. One day, in the middle of a lesson on the quadratic formula, Brad gently removed the freshly sharpened number two pencil from Thena's fingers, placed it on his one-subject notebook, and kissed her hand. When she didn't pull away, he leaned in for a kiss on the lips, one that would go down in history as *the kiss that shook the planet.* Or at least that was how Brad's best man phrased it during the wedding toast. Because seconds after Brad kissed Thena in the library that day, Southern Cali experienced a magnitude-three earthquake. It was so subtle that they thought the unexpected trembling of their table and bookshelves was, in fact, an aftershock from their first kiss, one that only the two of them could feel.

In the past, a love story like this would have inspired me. I probably would have already written up a bridge or a chorus to a love song before my second glass of wine. The unsettling truth, however, is that hearing Thena's happily-ever-after of a love story is like rubbing margarita salt into an open wound.

"So that's about it," she says with a sigh. "We went to two separate colleges, which was challenging to say the least, but we survived by the skin of our teeth. We were engaged soon after graduation and had Oakley two years later."

"That's, wow, that's just so great," I say, pouring more wine into my glass. "I love happy endings."

"How about you?" she asks, the slight hesitation in her voice not going unnoticed. "I mean, I know what the magazine article says… and Twitter… and Instagram… and…" Her voice trails off.

"I haven't read the article, and I've stayed off social, so I don't know what it says." I cringe, wondering how much wine needs to be in my system before I cave and begin stalking Victor on Insta.

"So, you legit just packed up and left two days ago? Did you leave a house behind? An apartment?"

Her questions cause my head to spin. Of course I left a home behind. A gorgeous one-bedroom open-concept luxury apartment in the Miracle Mile neighborhood, one of LA's most desirable places to live, or at least I thought so. And no, I didn't give any thought to how I would pack up the last eight years of my life. But thank you, Thena, for reminding me.

"Yeah," I say, staring out the window and peering up at the stars. "I left my apartment behind. Paid the rent for the next three months and hopped on the first flight I could." I wince, annoyed at myself for spending what was the last of my savings on three months of rent.

"Wow, three months?"

"Yeah. I guess I just didn't want to have to worry about packing." My cheeks turn pink, and I run my fingers through my hair.

"And Victor? Did you even get to say goodbye?"

My eyes grow wide, and I shake my head. "No. There was no goodbye."

"What the *hell* happened?"

I shift nervously on my barstool. I open my mouth to speak, but nothing comes out. "It's a lot," I finally say.

"I'm sorry. I shouldn't have asked."

"No," I say, reassuringly. "It's okay. I'm the one who said I wanted to clear my name. It's just hard. Everything happened so fast, and I honestly don't even know where I would begin."

"Well," she says with a sigh, "the beginning is always a great place to start."

"It is, isn't it?" I agree. "It's just a really long story," I say, pulling the magazine out of my bag. I trace my fingers over the image of Victor's face as he stares up at me from the cover, my heart surely bleeding out from inside my body, and for a moment, I decide that there isn't anything I wouldn't do to take back what happened. *I had my own rules, too, Victor. And they changed because of you.* I furrow my brow and wipe away another tear, trying with all my might to remove that conversation from my brain. "I'm so tired of crying," I say with a laugh. But it isn't a happy laugh, and this seems to bother Thena.

She tilts her head to the side and studies me for a beat. "It's interesting," she says, passing me a clean napkin from the bar.

"What's interesting?"

"Love. It's never as simple as it appears to be, right?"

I nod, the tears flowing freely now. I peek down at the headline once more, and my stomach turns. "I don't need to read this," I say between sobs, "to know that what it says is *completely* wrong."

Thena takes my hand in hers and nods reassuringly. "You don't have to talk about it if you aren't ready, Summer."

I nod in agreement. "Yes," I say. "Yes, I do. It's time I get it out. Just promise me you aren't a news reporter or a member of the paparazzi," I say with a laugh. "I'm kidding but not kidding."

"OMG, me? I wish. That would really be cool. No, the only people I could possibly tell right now are Oakley and Brad, and he's so hyper focused on production and is only speaking of that. Oakley barely knows one hundred words, which is advanced, according to our pediatrician. I'm thankful for that because the other toddlers in our playgroup seem to have experienced significant gains in their gross and small motor development, more so than Oakley over the past few months. I try not to worry about it, but you want your kids to be the best they can be, you know? Not like I'm comparing her to them. I just want to know I'm a good mom."

"That answer," I say between sniffles, "is proof enough for me that you are who you say you are."

"Perfect."

"Okay," I say, exhaling louder and fuller than I mean to. "Hold on tight, Thena. You might want to grab yourself another margarita. We're gonna be here a while."

CHAPTER SEVEN

JULY 15, 2023

RIVER FROST

I should have offered to buy her a drink. Why didn't I offer to buy her a drink? I shake my head at my empty motel room and toss my take-out bag on the counter of the kitchenette, contemplating whether I should go back to the Sea-Pub and chill with Summer. She looked so lonely, sitting there by herself. Had she been crying? "Not your problem, River," I say out loud to the darkness. I flick on the light and remove a take-out container from the paper bag. "Lord knows you have your own share of problems."

I head to the fridge and crack open a Corona Light, not able to sit and eat my food fast enough. The day had gone well, and my director, Brad, was overly thankful for my retrieval of Lawson from the Anderson cottage. We had successfully filmed the scenes planned for the day and would be moving on to more of Lawson's scenes tomorrow, and because of that, I instructed him to be ready for me to pick him up at 7 a.m.

I sip my beer and reach for the magazine I had purchased on the way home from work. It was the first tabloid I have ever purchased, and I was so embarrassed upon buying it at the gas station that I loaded the counter with countless chips, candy bars, and Coronas just to make the magazine less visible on the counter.

I study the cover, like a scientist analyzing the results of an experiment. The headlines clearly state that the man Summer is kissing is her manager, Victor. But when I spoke with Blake last week, he insisted that the media magnified her situation, and in his words, this was *fake news*. But if this information was inaccurate, why did she rush home so quickly? I need to get to the bottom of this, and I need to start now. "What happened to you out there, Summer?" I ask the magazine cover. And without further hesitation, I flip the pages open to page twenty-four, eager to read what the press has to say about Summer Jennings and Victor Diaz, and I trace the headline with my pointer finger.

VICTOR DIAZ HAS a new Favorite Season—Summer

Talent manager and record producer Victor Diaz, 42, got steamy with recording artist and client Summer Jennings, 32, at the Rise 2 Fame reunion party on Thursday evening. So what? you might ask. What's the big deal? We've got the tea, and we're ready to spill it.

Sources say that Victor and Summer have been cohabitating for years. That's right, America. Flash back six years to the finals of Rise 2 Fame when Victor used his only save on Summer after she received the least number of votes in the top five. The couple shared a heated embrace that won the hearts of millions, but was it innocent? Or did she get his vote simply because they were sleeping together?

Not only does this discredit Summer's win on Rise 2 Fame, but it also puts a dark and stormy cloud over Victor and his once squeaky-clean reputation. Why? Well, maybe because of his four-year-long engagement to Nova Moore. That's why.

Dozens of fans have spoken out on Rise 2 Fame about Victor's betrayal of Nova and about Summer's cheating scandal. Summer, Victor, and Nova have all refused to comment. Rumor has it Summer's 2024 tour has been postponed until allegations can be further investigated.

I SHAKE my head from side to side, growing even more curious about Summer and her situation, but my thoughts are interrupted by the buzzing of my cell, and seeing Kinsley's beautiful face flash on my screen is enough to cause me to toss the magazine to the side and save the Hollywood drama for another day. I wipe my mouth with a napkin and swipe open the FaceTime call, eager to see her face and hear her voice.

PART TWO

JULY EIGHTH

ONE WEEK EARLIER

CHAPTER EIGHT

JULY 8, 1994

MILLIE BIRD-JENNINGS

I was savoring the last sip of my favorite wine when we realized Summer was missing. It had been a lovely evening on the porch with Al. We often shared a glass of my favorite red, Caymus cabernet sauvignon, and reminisced about a time long ago when it felt like he and I were the only two people in the world. We held hands and listened carefully to the serenity of Long Sands Beach in the evening. The rhythmic pattern of the waves crashing seemed to be in sync with the rocking of our chairs, and from the Anderson cottage's third floor, the sky was a blanket of stars. The sky's visibility on that night was truly remarkable. Al and I had spotted both Ursa Major, the Big Dipper, and Ursa Minor, the Little Dipper, prior to Lark bursting through the sliding door and out onto the porch.

I remember it as clear as day. I had just checked my watch and realized that it was well after nine o'clock p.m., and by that time, I would have normally tucked the girls into bed, and Al would have been heading downstairs for his cigar with Gerry. Before heading outside with Al, I had instructed Summer to put on her nightgown and reminded Lark that there was no television after nine o'clock. But it was Lark who barged through the doors, taking us both by surprise. Her presence filled our small hideaway with a sense of urgency.

"She's not out here?" Lark asked, her eyes darting from Al to myself and back to Al.

"Who?" Al asked, concern rising in his voice.

"Summer! She's not in her bed."

I lost Violet in a shopping mall once. She was about six years old and thought it would be funny to hide in a clothing rack while I paced around the women's department, screaming her name. I never forgot what that felt like, and in that moment, when I heard that Summer was not in her bed or in the living room, I was taken directly back to that day. My knees grew weak, and my insides flipped around and around from the deepest parts of me. I leapt from my chair, dropping my wineglass and not even pausing to see if it survived the fall. "Are you sure?" I asked, my voice coming out as a choked whisper.

"I'm sure, Birdie."

"Stay calm," Al directed, bending down to scoop up the broken pieces of glass with a plastic beach shovel. "She's got to be here somewhere."

But she wasn't. Summer was nowhere to be found. Lark insisted that she last saw her changing into her nightgown, grabbing a snack from the kitchen, and heading to bed with her favorite stuffed kitten, Marvin. But Summer was not in her bed. Instead, in the spot where my precious little grand-daughter should have been snuggled up and sleeping soundly were only her pillow and Marvin the cat. "Call the police, Al!" I shouted. The blood rose to my face, and the room began to spin. I could hear the panicked sound of Lark calling out for her sister.

"I'll check the beach," she called to us, already running out of the Anderson cottage before I could object. I shook my head from side to side, trying with all my might to shake panicked thoughts from my terrified mind. *The beach. The ocean.*

I sprinted down the narrow hallway and began searching for her like my life depended on it. I started in the bathroom, frantically searching the linen closet, then the bathtub, and even the hamper, crying, "Summer! Summer, this isn't funny young lady!" I could hear Al on the phone with the police. Fear and dread filled my mind as I started downward spiraling, trying desperately not to think of the horrible things that could have happened to her. "Summer!" I called again, this time flinging the door to my own bedroom open. I pulled back the bedspread, searched under the bed, and tore through closets. My knees grew weaker as I caved to the panic. I collapsed on my bed and began sobbing with my face in my hands, the tears flowing out of my eyes with increasing intensity, a hot and salty river flowing down my cheeks. *Think, Millie!* I silently scolded. Where on earth could she have gone? Who, if anyone, would have taken her?

Long Sands Beach was certainly a safe place, and we had been staying at the Anderson cottage for years. The first floor of the cottage was currently vacant, and the second floor was occupied only by Gerry and... Sean. *Sean.* My thoughts raced back to a conversation I'd overheard earlier that day. Summer had begged Sean to teach her the guitar. I leapt to my feet and made my way to the corner of my bedroom as fast as my bare feet could carry me. Sure enough, there in between the oak dresser and the antique rocking chair, where my black-leather guitar case typically rested, was nothing but an empty space. I double-checked under the bed to make sure I hadn't tucked it away after playing it the previous night, and just as I thought, nothing.

I darted down the hallway of the cottage, past Al as he

stood against the kitchen wall, bracing the phone like a lifeline, trapped by its plastic spiral cord, his eyebrows risen in confusion.

"I know where she is!" I shouted, not pausing to offer any explanation. I bolted down the stairs and rounded the corner just in time to see Lark running from the beach.

"I didn't find her!" she cried.

"It's okay!" I said, not sure if I was reassuring Lark or myself. "I think I know where she is. Come on," I instructed as I approached the sliding door to the second floor of the Anderson cottage and began banging my fists against the sliding door's glass.

"Sean!" Lark called. "Sean, open up!"

I wrapped my arm around Lark's waist and pulled her close. What felt like years later, Sean appeared at the porch door, his guitar in hand and eyes wide. "Is she here?" I cried out. "Summer! Is she here?"

"Yes," he said, confusion washing over him. "She brought your guitar downstairs just a few minutes ago. She told me you said—"

"Summer?" I yanked the door open farther and searched the kitchen with wide eyes. There, perched on the surface of the table next to my open guitar case, was my granddaughter, Summer. She sat cross-legged on the kitchen table in her bright-pink-and-teal Care Bears nightgown, holding my guitar—a 1959 Gibson J-200 maple-finish acoustic. It appeared enormous on her tiny body but not as gigantic as the smile on her face as she strummed the strings of my guitar, surely mimicking my movements from the previous night.

"We were just coming to get you, Birdie," Gerry says with a snicker as he rounded the corner of the living room to the kitchen, cigar in hand. "Little Summer here came downstairs a few minutes ago, asking Sean to teach her guitar."

"I'm so sorry, Birdie," Sean said, shaking his head from side to side. "I thought it was strange that it was so late and she was by herself, but she told me you wanted her to come down and that she could come back up with Grandpa Gerry for cigars."

My eyes darted to Summer's, and by the look of her tiny pout and watery eyes, she knew she was in for it. "Summer!" I scolded. "What were you thinking? We thought we lost you!"

I half expected her to remain silent, but she pressed her cheek to the body of my guitar and squeezed it like she normally squeezed Marvin the cat. "Lark said that when Sean plays the guitar, it's an escape to heaven." Her bottom lip quivered, and she burst into tears. "I'm sorry, Birdie. I wanted to escape to heaven."

"Baby girl," I cried, rushing over to her. I removed the guitar from her hands and placed it in on the table before reaching for her and scooping her up into my arms. Her sniffles turned to sobs, and the wetness of her tears filled the crevice of my neck. "You *never* leave the cottage without telling us. Do you understand?"

"But I didn't leave the cottage," she cried. "I just went downstairs."

"You know what I mean," I said, my tone firm.

"Okay, Birdie."

"I'll teach you guitar, beautiful girl. Just not tonight."

She peeked up at me and wiped her wet and matted tresses out of her eyes. "But..." Her voice trailed off.

"But what?"

"You don't know Guns N' Roses. I want to learn how to play Guns N' Roses."

Laughter erupted from around us, and it was only then that I realized Al had found us. "Summer Rose!" he said, making his way toward us and pulling her from me. "You gave us quite the scare."

"I'm sorry, Papa," she said, clinging to his neck for what looked like dear life. "I wanted to play the guitar with Sean Anderson."

"Is that right?" Al asked, his own voice catching in his throat. "Don't ever do that again. Do you understand?" My husband wiped a tear from the corner of his eye and kissed her once more.

"I understand."

"Whenever life gets hard, Summer, you know you can always turn to Birdie and me. We are always here for you."

Lark squeezed through Al and me and wrapped her arm around her sister's waist. "You scared me, you little twerp," she said, her words harsh but her tone filled with genuine concern.

Al wrapped his arm around Lark's waist and pulled her close, pressing her up against Summer's tiny body as she dangled in his arms. Summer reached down and wrapped her hand around Lark's finger, and my heart melted. *How wonderful to have a sister,* I thought. Surely, they will always have each other.

"I'm sorry, Lark," Summer whispered in the stillness of the kitchen.

"It's okay. I love you, you know?"

"I love you too."

"Do it again, though, and I'll kick your tiny butt all the way to the moon."

CHAPTER NINE

JULY 8, 2023

SUMMER ROSE JENNINGS

There was a time when all I wanted was to teach music to children. I did, in fact, come close to making that dream a reality. It was senior year of college when my roommate, Tessa Walker, submitted a recording to *Rise 2 Fame*, a nationwide singing competition. Tessa, who could have completed undergrad with her eyes closed and her hands tied behind her back, was given the pleasure of listening to me complain about the basic core classes necessary to graduate with a degree and a teaching certificate. When the opportunity to compete in a singing competition came across her Facebook page, she knew that the show could be the answer to all of my life's greatest problems.

I was *never* one of the smart kids. I excelled in any music-related class, but the frustration and anxiety I experienced in high school math, science, and history were enough to convince me to take a year off before college. It was then that I saved money by cleaning motel rooms for my family's business and helping with my younger brother, Blake. It was only when I grew tired of working for the motel, especially during the offseason, that I applied to Plymouth State University, eager to put my past behind me and try something new.

Taking a year off before college was just what I needed. Not only did it allow time to reflect on what was truly important to me, but it also helped me to realize what I did *not* want for my life. That alone gave me the drive I needed to take my college studies seriously enough to make it through. Once I started taking music and child-development courses, I was truly in my element.

It was the end of the summer following graduation when everything changed. I was minutes away from signing my teaching contract when the producers of *Rise 2 Fame* called. I was sitting on a bench overlooking the Nubble Lighthouse, watching the waves crash along the rocky coastline as I often did. Blake and his friend had walked to get ice cream, and I was eagerly awaiting their return so I could drive them home. I had a meeting scheduled with the principal of a local elementary school to sign my teaching contract, and I didn't want to be late. I almost didn't answer the call, as it was a number and area code that weren't familiar to me. Maybe if I had known that Tessa submitted the video, I would have answered on the first ring. But in true Tessa fashion, she didn't tell me she'd submitted the video. So, when the producer called to welcome me as part of the cast for the 2015 season, I was shocked, to say the least.

I wish I could say that my family had been supportive to hear the news that their daughter was on her way to stardom. Maybe it was because we would forever be in debt with student loan payments as a result of my college years. Or it could have been because of the horror stories they'd read about actresses and artists going out to Hollywood and ending up being chewed up and spit out by the entertainment industry.

"You're going to end up making those sex movies," my

father had accused me upon receiving the news of my sudden career change.

I had crossed my arms over my chest and stomped my foot like a toddler having a tantrum. "You mean porn? Dad, I'm not going to be a porn star! Seriously, you are *so* embarrassing!" I had stormed away from them, slamming my bedroom door behind me.

It was my grandmother, Birdie, who had been the most supportive of my news. It was also Birdie who calmed my parents down long enough for them to look over the *Rise 2 Fame* contract. After passing it along to their lawyer and investigating things further, they allowed their little girl, their middle child, the freedom to explore her dreams.

I did more than explore my love for music, though. I soared through the first month of the show's pretaping with ease. By the time we made it to the live shows featuring the top twenty contestants, I was a judges' favorite. One judge in particular, record producer and talent manager Victor Diaz, a very handsome man in his midthirties, took an extra special liking to me. Some of the fans and cast members joked that he had a crush on me.

"He's ten years older than me," I would rebut. "Gross."

Twenty contestants dwindled down to fifteen then ten and then five. During the live voting reducing the top five contestants to the top three, I was almost voted off. I was given an opportunity to sing one song in hopes that a judge would use their save on me. My version of "Make You Feel My Love" on piano was enough for Victor Diaz to use his only save of the season. I had been so emotional, so caught off guard, so overwhelmed, and so grateful that I all but leapt off the stage to where he was seated at the judges' table. I wrapped my arms around him and cried, "Thank you!" My words lost themselves in his neck's crevice.

"You earned this," he said. "Don't ever forget that. You're a star."

My save made headlines, especially since Victor's words of praise were picked up through his microphone, and it was only weeks later that I was declared the winner of *Rise 2 Fame*. My entire family—including my grandmother, grandfather, and siblings—attended the finale. It had been the best night of my life by far, and it was only the beginning. Soon after the show wrapped up, I joined the rest of the top ten contestants for a nationwide tour. Life could not have been better. That was, until Victor reached out to me personally, declaring that once my contract was up with *Rise 2 Fame*, he would like to be my manager.

The next six years went by in a flash. Victor promised me that I would have my own tour in no time, and he kept his promise and more. With his production company, I recorded my first album, which climbed the charts faster than any of us thought possible. I began opening for my favorite artists and before long had a tour of my own. My tour wrapped up in 2021, and it was after that that I settled into the apartment of my dreams, a one-bedroom 857-square-foot luxury space with a rooftop pool and bar.

The rooftop pool quickly became my favorite spot. And on that day, as I lay perched on a lounge chair, under the shade of an umbrella, in my favorite magenta bikini, notebook on lap, sipping raspberry-lime seltzer, I decided I was probably the luckiest girl in the world.

"What's up, Sums!"

I looked up from my notebook to see Victor approaching. He carried a large brown paper bag and a bottle of water in one hand, a black-leather computer bag draped over his shoulder. His long-sleeved black button-down shirt was completely unbuttoned, and I tried with all my might to look away from the eight-pack that poked through beneath his deep-olive skin, but *damn*. Nearly impossible. "How did you know where to find me?" I asked sarcastically.

"If you weren't up here, I would be worried."

"Noted," I said, twisting my brunette tresses up into a messy bun and adjusting my bikini top.

"Writing your next hit?" he asked, gesturing to my notebook.

"Actually, it's my grocery list," I said with a wink.

"Sure, it is," he chuckled, taking a seat next to me and opening the bag. "Got your favorite."

"You didn't!"

"I did."

"Thank you," I said, wrapping my arms around his neck, pausing for longer than probably appropriate, but I didn't care. I inhaled his sweet, musky scent, wanting to bottle it up and store it away. I pulled back and smiled, immediately at ease and just happy to be in his company.

If I haven't made it obvious enough, Victor had become my favorite person on the planet, but in my defense, that didn't just happen overnight. What had started as a professional relationship had turned into more of a family dynamic over the years. Being alone out in California, with my parents back home, had been hard, to say the least. Victor, being ten years older than me, acted like an older brother at times, which was just what I needed. When he got engaged to his girlfriend, Nova, I was worried that might change, but he consistently continued to make time for me, look out for me, and well, just take care of me, referring to me as his best friend. Now, as I sat with him by the pool, eating my favorite —a BLT sub with American cheese and extra mayo—I found that I couldn't actually stop smiling. That was, until Victor dropped a tabloid magazine onto my chair and pointed at the headline—*Cold Feet?*

Victor sighed and kicked off his sneakers. "Never a dull

moment, huh?" He grunted, tossing his sneakers to the side of the chair.

The media had a field day because of Victor's four-year-long engagement to his fiancée. Nova was a swimsuit model, of course, and had appeared in such magazines as *Vogue, Sports Illustrated, Maxim*, and *Vanity Fair*, to name a few. Not only was she popular for her success in the industry, but it was also her social media influence and initiatives within black women's empowerment that declared her America's sweetheart—partnering with *Vogue* and Black Women's Health Imperative for one. She was stunning, fit, smart, and lovable. Everyone was captivated by Nova. Even those secretly envious of her loved her. Her stunning, muscular, long, defined legs seemed to go on for miles. Her bouncy, spirally golden tresses seemed to take on a life of their own and complemented her personality in a way that constantly drew people in. When Victor was asked why he and Nova had yet to set a date for their wedding, he would laugh and redirect the question to her, emphasizing that she was the one in charge, not him.

That was probably the most accurate thing Victor could have said. Because just two weeks prior, out of nowhere, Nova had decided to call off their engagement. It was a decision she made on her own, coming out of a conversation they had over dinner, one that included questions about when and if they would have children. In the past, Victor had been convinced that having children was not at the top of his priority list but had since changed his mind, as he had recently experienced becoming an uncle. Nova, on the other hand, knew with one-hundred-percent certainty that being a mother was not in the cards for her. Victor begged her to reconsider, but she remained firm in her decision, convinced that this was nonnegotiable. It was a messy breakup, but as angry as Victor was, he completely understood. Nova had begged Victor to keep this new development private for now, leaving the public to believe that the happy couple was indeed still together, even though their relationship was very much over.

"That's bullshit," I said, tracing a finger over the headline. "When are you going to let the cat out of the bag?"

"Probably never," he said before taking a bite of his sandwich. "Nova is working on a book deal, and breaking off the engagement with me will result in a loss in followers. And I still might try to win her back."

"Oh yeah? How do you plan on doing that?" I flipped the magazine open to the article. I scanned it with my eyes and looked up at him in disbelief. "Wow, Victor, you are…"

"The nicest guy ever? I win the most supportive ex-fiancé award?"

"No. I was going to say you're a pushover."

Victor cleared his throat and reached for his water. "Thanks."

"Just keeping it real." I punched him playfully in the shoulder. "Seriously, though. I don't see Nova budging on this one. How are you doing with all of this?"

He considered this for a moment. "I understand why she did it. It just doesn't make it hurt any less," he confessed.

"I can't imagine it would."

"Anyway, what do you have going on for the rest of the day?"

"I have a hair appointment and then a dress fitting for next week."

"The big party," he said, nodding his head.

"Yup, I'm old enough to be a *Rise 2 Fame* alumni. I've never felt so old."

"Thirty-two is not old, Summer."

"Getting there," I say with a smile. "And if I'm old, you're *really* old."

"Is that what your hair appointment is for? Covering up the grays?" he asked, tickling my side.

His touch sent tiny electric shocks through my body, forcing me to shift uncomfortably in my seat. I adjusted my sunglasses over my eyes in hopes I could disguise the range of emotions and feelings that flooded within me. For years, my friendship with Victor had been nothing but professional, and any sort of feelings were those of gratitude in a sisterly sort of way. So why now was it getting impossible to ignore? Could it have been because of the breakup? I had always adored Nova and never would have done anything to come between her and Victor. Was it because I hadn't been out on a date in over a year?

"You good?" he asked.

"Why wouldn't I be?" I asked with a smile. "You're going, right? To the party?"

"Hells, yeah," he said, high-fiving me. "It'll be my first night out as a single man."

"Yeah." I chuckled. "Except according to all of your adoring fans, you're still engaged," I said, my tone matching his and holding my hand out for a high five.

"Cute, Summer. Real cute."

"Come on," I said, standing up and turning toward the pool. "This is Hollywood. The drama will always be there. Let's go for a swim," I said, pulling his hands in mine and yanking him off the chair.

"I don't really feel like swimming, Sum." Victor removed his shirt and tossed it onto the ground.

"Oh no?"

"No. My heart is too broken," he said, a smile forming on the corner of his lips. He stepped out of his shorts, revealing navy-blue-and-black swim shorts.

"I'm sorry," I said, playing along. "I've never had my heart broken. I wish I could help, but I've got nothing." I turned, prepared to dive into the pool, expecting Victor to be behind me. But in one swoop of his arms, Victor picked me up and swung me over his shoulder, his skin feeling warm against my bare stomach.

"Victor!" I cried through my laughter.

"Cannonball!" he cheered midair, heaving our bodies into the pool.

My feet hit the water first, the rush of coldness both invigorating and startling. I closed my eyes and welcomed the rush of adrenaline through my body as I was pulled down to the bottom and then back up again, gasping for air and rubbing my eyes.

"Jerk," I said, making a fist and pounding on his chest. But what I meant was, "Could we do that again? And again tomorrow, and the next day, and the day after that? Because I don't know what's going on between us, Victor Diaz, but I do know that whatever it is, whatever it means, I sure as hell do like it a lot."

CHAPTER TEN

JULY 8, 2023

RIVER FROST

It had been two weeks since I first settled in at the Seabird. Blake had been more than accommodating, hooking up me and the rest of the production team with extended-stay rooms. I had learned a lot about Blake's family just through conversation with residents of the town and people I'd met at the Sea-Pub but also because he really liked to talk. His grandparents Birdie and Al started their family business in the early sixties and then handed it over to their daughter and her husband just a little over five years ago. They also had a daughter who lived in Florida, where they resided in the summer, and then of course their middle daughter, Summer, was a celebrity and famous recording artist who lived out in LA.

Blake liked to talk about his family. He was very proud of the Seabird and its success. His grandmother's oatmeal cookie recipe was what he prided himself on the most. He baked them himself in his apartment above the main office and handed out at least two dozen a day. I was pretty sure his cookie motivations were not always pure, as his good-boy grandson baking routine got him laid on occasion, and I was pretty sure he at times concocted some "special" cookies for him and his friends—but that was a story for another day.

I burrowed my toes farther into the warmth of the sand and leaned back onto my elbows. Blake approached, kicking up sand as he walked, his toothy white grin larger than usual as he dropped his own surfboard next to mine and reached into his cooler for beer. "Want one?" he asked, but he'd already passed it to me, knowing the answer.

"Thanks, man," I said, brushing sand off my fingers and onto my legs and cracking the beer open. This had been my first and only day off since we started filming *The Hundredth Time Around*. It wasn't a scheduled day off. There had been technical difficulties locating the 1942 Cadillac necessary for Gerry and Gwendoline's Nubble Lighthouse scenes, along with some United States Navy paraphernalia that wasn't quite right. That, paired with the fact that older Joey Chase had come down with a bad head cold, was enough for Brad to finally cancel the day of filming. "It feels so good to do nothing," I said, nodding to Blake and swigging my beer.

"Tell me about it," he said with a sigh. "My parents finally just left for Florida, so I feel like I can breathe." He ran his fingers through his wet brunette tresses.

"Are they hard to work for?"

"Nah, they're harmless. They're good people."

"They sound like it," I said, staring out at the breaking waves. "It's good to have family around." I thought about this for a beat, rubbing my jaw with my fingers in an effort to elevate the tension, suddenly wanting to drive into Boston and sweep Kinsley off her feet this very second.

"Your family back in Cali?" he asked, taking a sip of his beer.

I hesitated for a moment, choosing my words carefully. "My mother and father are out in California, yes."

"Siblings?"

"Nope."

"Girlfriend?"

"Nope."

"My sister is out in California," he said, and I stopped and wondered if he forgot mentioning Summer to me a handful of times already. "She's Summer Jennings," he said, eyes wide. "You know, Summer Jennings from *Rise 2 Fame*."

Convinced he tells this story so often to so many people, I decided to simply smile. "You don't say?"

"Aw, man, did I already tell you about her?" he asked with a laugh.

"Don't sweat it," I said. "Does she ever come back home? Summer?"

"Nah, she's making it big out there. She's already planning her next tour. Why? Are you a fan or something?"

I smiled at this. "Me? No. But I know someone who is. Do you think she would autograph something for me?"

"Is your *girlfriend* into her or something?" he asked, the corners of his mouth curving up into a smile.

"Like I said, I don't have a girlfriend."

"We should fix that, then," he said, gesturing toward a group of girls I assumed to be his age. There were four of them sprawled out on beach towels, each wearing the same high-waisted two-piece bathing suit but in different colors and patterns.

"Thanks, but no thanks," I said, standing up and brushing the sand off my legs. "They're at least ten years younger than me."

"How old are you?"

"Old enough." I sighed, attempting to avoid any talk of age, seeing as though my thirty-third birthday was coming up, and I would most likely be spending it on set or alone.

"You sure? You can't be much older than them. I hooked up with the redhead my senior year of high school and—"

"Positive," I said, slapping him playfully on his back. "Go get 'em, tiger."

"So, are you married or something? Do you have a wife? Is she the one who wants the autograph? Or wait, do you have a boyfriend? No judgment, man. My best friend was into guys, and I was totally cool with it."

"You sure do ask a lot of questions, Blake Jennings," I said, tossing the empty beer can back into his cooler and reaching for my surfboard. "Just have her make the autograph out to Kinsley. I would bet any amount of money that she is without a doubt Summer's biggest fan."

CHAPTER ELEVEN

JULY 8, 2023

SUMMER ROSE JENNINGS

I was touching up my lipstick in the bathroom mirror at the *Rise 2 Fame* reunion party when it hit me like a ton of bricks. *I'm in love with Victor Diaz.* The thought ricocheted through my brain faster than the speed of light, immediately followed by a wave of unexpected nausea so strong that I gripped the sides of the sink in an effort to hold myself up and not vomit.

I wished I knew why these feelings were suddenly so overbearing. I had originally thought that because of his breakup with Nova, my mind was playing tricks on me. Maybe my interest in him had been because he was the only person I spent any sort of time with. But as my stylist had painted my maroon highlights onto my hair earlier that week and we talked about nothing but everything, I found myself saying Victor's name more than usual. *Victor* signed a new child actress who, at the age of five, had over 1.5 million followers on Instagram. *Victor* tried the new chocolate-cold-foam cold brew from Starbucks and said it was freaking incredible. *Victor* suggested the maroon highlights for the photo shoot next week. Victor. Victor. Victor.

I adjusted the black satin fabric of my strapless dress and studied my reflection in the mirror. He had been totally right about the highlights. They were perfect. But the uneasy nervous feeling that was developing in my gut was unfamiliar, because suddenly, I couldn't wait for Victor to see my highlights. I couldn't wait for Victor to see *me*.

Of course, Victor and I could never be a thing. Age difference aside, he was like a brother to me. I also couldn't deny the fact that even though his and Nova's engagement was called off, Victor was determined to get her back. I wanted him to be happy, and if getting back together with Nova would make him happy, then that was what I wished for him.

But if I was really pushing for Nova and Victor to get back together, then why did I feel the way I was feeling now? Why did it suddenly seem like my insides were going to explode outside of me and I would explode into a million pieces if I didn't get the validation that I needed from Victor? Why, suddenly, was it a life-or-death that I needed him to feel the same way? I rummaged through my clutch and retrieved my cell.

Summer: Artist-Hinder

Tessa: Song?

Summer: Lips of an Angel. Acoustic version.

MY TEXT WAS CUT short because my phone was vibrating, and I was receiving a FaceTime call from Tessa. I balanced my clutch under my arm and scooted into a stall, quickly checking for feet underneath the doors and deciding this setting was private enough to take a call. I flipped the toilet seat down and sat before swiping open the call from Tessa.

"Hi," I said, warm relief flooding over me like sunshine on

a cloudy day. "It's good to see your face. Hawaii agrees with you." Tessa's skin was sun-kissed, and her dark hair was up in a messy bun. She wore a royal-blue tankini and large Ray-Ban sunglasses. "Sorry," I said with a sigh. "I forgot about the six-hour difference again. Are you busy with Bex?"

"No worries at all," Tessa said with a smile. "It's one p.m. here. Bex and Desmond are out surfing. I was just hanging back doing some research. This wedding planning is no joke. But in other news, you look stunning. I love your hair!"

"Thanks," I said, checking out my new hairdo on my phone's screen. "It's kind of a big night."

"That's right. The reunion party."

"Yes."

"So, I haven't heard 'Lips of an Angel' in a while, so you're going to have to clarify. I know it's about wanting someone you can't have, but I can't quite put my finger on who you would be referring to unless…"

"Shhh," I said, holding my finger up to my lips and glancing under the stall.

Tessa whispered "Victor," and I nodded, scrunching my face up in agony.

"I don't know what's happening, Tessa. I've known him for so long, and I know it isn't going to happen, but suddenly, he's the only person I can think about. Someone at the dress fitting this afternoon smelled like him, and I couldn't complete a freaking sentence. I feel like an actual stalker."

"You're not a stalker," she said with a smile.

"Is there some kind of clinical term you know of, like I could be projecting my feelings of gratitude toward him and it feels like a crush because he's so freaking great and I don't want to lose him?"

She thought for a moment. "Well, yes. But you know yourself, Summer. And I have a feeling this didn't just come out of nowhere."

I sighed, wiping a tear from the corner of my eye. "Well, regardless of what this *is*, I know what it's not. I know that it isn't going to happen. I'm just having a hard time coming to terms with the fact that I'm imagining this. He was so flirty the other day by the pool."

"He was?"

"Yes, and I know it wasn't my imagination."

"What did he do?"

"Well, first, he brought me my favorite sandwich, then after complaining about Nova, he tickled me and threw me in the pool."

"What is he, five years old?"

"Seriously."

"Actually, I went through something similar to this when I met Desmond for the first time."

"Really?"

"Really. I knew there was a connection, but there were just so many things I couldn't wrap my mind around. I couldn't tell if he was flirting or if it was just his personality."

"How did you know it was something?"

"He asked me out. I told him it wasn't a date. We were in his bed within the hour."

"Wow, Tessa, that's your typical fairy tale."

"It was more than that." She laughed. "But you owe it to yourself to address it with him. Maybe not tonight but soon. It sounds like he's sending you mixed signals for sure."

"Right? Ugh, I must go out there now, or they're going to send a search party."

"Go have fun, Summer. Put something happier on that playlist of yours."

"Like what?"

"You're the music guru." She laughed.

"Give me something. Anything."

"'Girl on Fire' by Alicia Keys."

"Perfect," I said, suddenly determined to have a fun night, with or without the validation that Victor could possibly ever feel the same way I did. Because deep down, I knew. My highlights were on point, my dress hugged my curves in all the right places, and in just six short years, I had managed to make all my dreams come true.

I exited the bathroom and scanned the venue for Victor.

"Summer!"

I whipped my head around toward the direction of my name to see Carly James, a fellow cast member from *Rise 2 Fame*, approaching me, one margarita in each hand.

"Carly," I said with a smile. "It's been so long."

"Not long enough to forget your favorite drink."

"Thank you," I said, clinking my glass to hers and taking a sip. "Here's to a great night," I cheered.

"The best! Drink up. I already have more coming!" she said as she danced away.

CHAPTER TWELVE

JULY 8, 2023

RIVER FROST

I leaned my elbows against the mahogany bar at the Sea-Pub.

"Night off tonight?" Ralph, a good-looking kid who probably turned twenty-one, twenty-one seconds ago, asked as he slid my second Corona Light in my direction.

"Yes, sir," I said with a nod. "First day off all summer and most likely my last." There was no way Brad was going to make this a habit, and I didn't blame him. We were behind schedule, which didn't bode well for the budget.

"And you're spending it here? At the Sea-Pub?" he asked, and I couldn't tell if he was judging me or the restaurant.

"I didn't have any better ideas." I shrugged. "Plus, I like it here. It's a good vibe," I said, taking a sip of my beer.

"Good to know," he said. "Are you alone up here? I've met a few families who tagged along with their spouses for the filming."

I nodded, thinking of Thena and Oakley, Brad's family. "Nah, I'm just a PA. They aren't going to pay to put my family up."

"Bummer."

That is the understatement of the century, I thought to myself. I would have given anything to have Kinsley here in Maine with me for the summer, but it just hadn't worked out the way we wanted it to. I had started making a list in the notepad of my phone of places I was convinced she would love. The Nubble Lighthouse, Long Sands Beach, Short Sands Beach, the piano bar, the candy store... The list went on and on, and every time I typed in it, my heart felt a little emptier, because it just wasn't going to happen.

When I had decided to take the PA position on the set of *The Hundredth Time Around*, I did so knowing that being away from Kinsley would be hard, to say the least. *But when you want something bad enough, especially in your career, you sacrifice, right?* And she had responsibilities and commitments back home in Boston too. I enjoyed being on set, and if being a PA was where I needed to start, then that was what I would do. Of course, I'd written script after script, and nothing had been picked up, and I was hoping the networking I had done coming out of film school would have progressed more than it had, but the truth was, I was stuck. Pushing for a director position at this point was the only practical option, and I couldn't do that unless I climbed the ladder, networked, and found myself in the right place at the right time.

I took the last sip of my drink and stared out the window of the Sea-Pub. The sun was setting, decorating the sky with strokes of pastel and golden yellow. 3 Doors Down's "Here Without You" played in the restaurant, and a sudden wave of sadness splashed over me, like the waves that crashed against the rocks outside. Yes, I missed Kinsley. I always missed Kinsley, but what was this other unfamiliar feeling of emptiness and hopelessness that was emanating through my veins? Why, suddenly, did I feel like I was in the opposite place that I needed to be? Was there an opposite of "right place right time"? Wouldn't it be "wrong place wrong time"? I decided that it was time to pay my tab and call it a night. I wasn't sure why I was feeling the way I was, but suddenly, getting out of there and heading to sleep was the only thing I could think of that felt like the right thing to do. But just as I pulled my debit card out of my pocket and began waving down Ralph to close out my tab, Blake took a seat on the stool next to me and declared that he would have one of what I was having and told the bartender to grab me another.

* * *

THREE HOURS LATER, the sun was long gone, and the view out the window of the Sea-Pub was nothing but darkness. Blake and I leaned over a high-top, enjoying the company of a few guys from the movie set who were ignoring Ralph's warning for last call, when Blake's phone started vibrating on the middle of the table. I recognized the photo on Blake's screen immediately—it was Summer Jennings, his sister. "Blake, your phone is ringing," I said, scooping up the phone and handing it across the table.

"Don't worry about it," he said, brushing me off.

"Not trying to be nosy, man, but I think it's your sister."

Blake gawked up at me in a drunken haze and mumbled, "You get it, then, if it's that important," and carried on his conversation.

The phone stopped vibrating, and the call ended. I plonked it back down in the center of the table, but sure enough, it began ringing again. "Blake, she's calling again." I raised it up in his direction, and he stumbled backward.

"I told you to answer it," he slurred, sliding the call open with his finger and shoving the phone in my face.

I rolled my eyes at him and raised the phone to my ear, silently cursing myself for sticking my nose where it didn't belong. I shook my head and hurried toward the nearest exit, relief flooding over me as the cool night's ocean air jostled me awake. What in the actual hell was I supposed to say to Summer Jennings? Man, would Kinsley lose her mind, knowing that I was about to have a conversation with her idol. Thoughts flew through my mind by the dozen, but in the end, all I could muster up was a simple, "Hello? Summer?"

I waited for what seemed like hours for a response, but the line remained silent. I checked the bars at the top of the screen, wondering if the connection was the issue, but the cell service seemed okay. "Hello?" I asked again.

"Blakey?" a hushed and timid voice poked through the line. Her words caught in her throat, and a few seconds passed before multiple sobs erupted through the phone into my ear. Was she crying?

"I'm coming home!" she wailed. "I… messed it up good."

Based on the way she was slurring her words, it was clear to me that she was just as drunk as her brother. Considering how upset she sounded and the state of mind they were both in, I decided to do the only thing I could think to do. I lied and pretended to be Blake.

"Why? What happened? Is everything okay?"

"No, Blakey, it isn't. Nothing is okay. I'm going to be flying home in just a few days, and I need a place to stay."

"I don't understand," I said, now pacing outside of the Sea-Pub and staring up at the starry sky. "Why do *you* need a place to stay? You have a place out in LA. Why would you need to come home?"

This caused her to wail so loudly that I pulled the phone from my ear and allowed myself a second to breathe. I placed the phone back in position only to realize her sobs had become deeper and heavier. "It's over. I messed it all up. They all hate me. Everyone is going to hate me. I need to get out of here. Please just tell me you have a place for me to stay, and if you say no, I'm calling Dad."

"Of course. Yeah, Summer, you have a place to stay. We have the extended-stay rooms at the Seabird for a reason, right?" I slapped my palm against my forehead and furrowed my brow.

"Really?" she sniffled. "Thank you. You really are the best brother in the world," she exclaimed, her drunken state causing her to sound like a child.

"Are you okay, though?" I asked, suddenly needing to know that she was going to be okay.

"It's a bad night. I've got some *sad* songs on my playlist, Blakey."

"I'm sorry to hear that," I said, a bit confused.

"I just don't know how I'm going to even get through this night!" Her sobs were coming out more freely now, like she had stopped trying to control them.

"Are you alone?" I asked, unsure of her relationship status or if she lived by herself.

"*So* alone."

I sighed, wondering how on earth I was supposed to help her. She thought I was Blake, for starters, so was that even my place? Was it wrong at that point to try to comfort her? The crying continued, and I heard the rustling of what sounded like keys, a door opening, a door closing, and a house alarm. I heard her punch in what sounded like four digits into an alarm pad, and the ringing subsided. "Are you home?"

"Yes."

I threw my head back and studied the night sky, remembering what I usually said to Kinsley when she felt alone and I wasn't there to comfort her. "Are you by a window?"

"Huh?"

"Are you by a window?"

"I live in a high-rise in LA. Of course I'm by a window, moron."

I heard what sounded like a sliding door open and then close. "Are you on a balcony?" I asked, suddenly nervous that because of me, she was standing alone on the balcony of her high-rise apartment.

"Yes."

"Be careful."

"Okay, *Dad.*" She snickered. "So why am I out here?"

"Look up at the sky."

"Okay, looking."

"How many stars do you see?"

"Um, I live in LA, butthead. Not many."

I laughed, suddenly feeling bad for Blake. In this short conversation, she had already referred to him as butthead and moron. No wonder he didn't want to answer her call. "Well, I'm counting now, and I'm estimating at least one hundred."

"I see a few. Why are we counting stars?"

"To prove to you, you aren't alone."

"Not following."

"We're looking up at the same night sky. I'm counting the same stars that you are counting. So technically, if we are under the same night sky, then you are never really as alone as you think you are."

She was silent for a moment, and I wondered if this resonated with her. I heard the sliding door open and close behind her. "I'll be home soon. Don't tell Mom and Dad yet… or anyone else."

"I won't."

"I don't know if I believe you." She sighed.

"Why not?"

"'Cause of the hamster."

I burst out laughing. "What?"

"The hamster, Blake. *Duh.* Good night."

And just like that, I was left standing outside of the Sea-Pub in the middle of the night, holding a cell phone that didn't belong to me, making promises I couldn't keep, and already trying to brainstorm ways to tell Blake Jennings that his celebrity sister was coming home to live at his family's motel.

CHAPTER THIRTEEN

JULY 8, 2023

SUMMER ROSE JENNINGS

I was on my third margarita when I spotted Victor from across the room. He was difficult to spot at first, considering most of the men at the party were wearing similar attire—black suit coats and black dress pants. Victor, however, wore a white button-down shirt and a silver tie underneath his jacket. I sipped the remaining drink from my glass, placed it on a nearby tray, and strutted over to him confidently. He was midsentence, speaking with a former *Rise 2 Fame* producer, when his eyes met mine. Maybe it was the tequila. Maybe it was just my imagination. But from my perspective, from where I was standing, Victor liked my highlights, and he liked *me*.

"Hey there," I said, leaning in for an embrace.

"What's up, Sums," he said, pulling me close to him. "You look gorgeous," he whispered.

His breath on my ear caused my heart to stop beating momentarily, and I cleared my throat in an effort to compose myself. "You look very nice too," I said, pulling back and smiling. But when I did, his eyes locked on mine, and a wave of electricity shot through my entire being. I realized my hand was still on his lower back. I flinched in embarrassment, moving back and allowing a few more inches between us.

"You okay?" he asked innocently enough.

"Me? Yeah, why wouldn't I be?"

"Just checking," he said, leaning in again for more secrets. "Love the hair."

I nodded and tucked a strand behind my ear. "Thanks," I mouthed, not sure if actual words were spoken out loud.

"What are you drinking?" he asked, studying the room for a server.

"Margaritas, what else," I said with a laugh.

"That's my girl." He winked, excusing himself from his previous conversation. "I'll go find you one."

I thanked him and retrieved my phone from my purse, deciding that this was a good time to text Tessa, because my brain was spiraling in confusion. And my heart, well, my heart was also spiraling in confusion but also pure joy. He liked my new hair and said I looked gorgeous. Surely, Tessa would need to know that I was no longer in crisis mode but having the time of my life with Victor and the best tequila buzz possible.

> Summer: Luke Bryan
>
> Tessa: Song?
>
> Summer: One Margarita 🍸
>
> Tessa: Nice. Have you seen him yet?
>
> Summer: Yes. This would be much easier if he was ugly and smelled bad.
>
> Tessa: LMAO. 😂😂 Have fun but behave. He isn't single yet. ‼

Victor returned with another margarita and a smile. I

tucked my phone away, taking the drink from him with gratitude and swigging faster than I normally would have. "Thank you," I said between sips.

"You sure you're good?" he asked, placing his hand on my lower back.

"Of course," I said, trying with all my might to keep my composure. But the more I drank, the better I felt. And the better I felt, the more honest I became with myself. And the more honest I became with myself, the more honest I wanted to be with Victor. But I couldn't be honest with Victor for a million reasons. And the more I drank, the sadder this made me feel. If there was ever a lose-lose situation, surely, this was it.

"I'm fine," I said, presenting him with the fakest smile imaginable. "Actually, I—"

But my words were cut short as someone cleared her throat from over his shoulder, and that someone was his ex-fiancée. "Nova!" I shrieked, mustering up every ounce of faux energy I could find deep in my soul. I nudged Victor and pointed at Nova, like he didn't understand the English language and needed a translator. "Look, Victor, it's Nova!"

Victor studied me like I had ten heads and greeted Nova with a long embrace. He closed his eyes and whispered something into her ear, and my happy trance instantaneously dissipated. I suddenly wanted to vomit. What was I thinking? What made me so convinced that I was as special to him as he was to me? The way he held her, the way he spoke to her in that moment, every ounce of confidence that was once shooting through me just minutes prior had evaporated into thin air. Every ounce of hope I had for Victor to ever see me as more than just his client had burst, and suddenly, my insides were screaming.

"Hi, Summer," Nova said, pulling me close and kissing me on the cheek. "It's so good to see you, darling."

"It's always good to see you, Nova," I said, pulling back from her and sipping my drink. The ground beneath my feet felt wobbly, and for a brief second, I regretted drinking so many margaritas. I reached out and grabbed onto Nova's hand for support, steadying my feet beneath me until I could regain my balance.

"Are you all right?" she asked, her tone full of concern.

"Yes," I said. "Silly me. I probably shouldn't have worn heels." I side glanced at Victor, who was not buying the wobbly-feet-from-the-heels act and placed his arm around Nova and kissed her on the cheek.

I'd never been sucker punched in the gut, but from what I could imagine, it would feel something like what I was experiencing in that very second. I gaped at Victor as he compressed his lips against Nova's face, and it sent me into an even deeper downward spiral of emotions. Of course he was going to kiss Nova. Not only was he in love with her, but they were also putting on a show for the media. Of course she was going to smile like she was the luckiest girl in the world—because she was. What I would have given to have Victor hold me like that, to kiss me like that, to… well, to *love* me like that.

I realized then that with one hundred percent of my entire being, I was in love with Victor Diaz. So much so that the sight of him standing behind his ex-fiancée, with his hands gripping her silver-metallic-sequinned twenty-three-inch waist, made me think that I was going to puke—or grab a flute of champagne from the nearest server, which I did. I reached for a champagne flute and shot it back in one quick movement, sucking it back like my life depended on it. I handed the empty glass to someone, not really sure who, and stared down at the ground, allowing the sugar rush to circulate through me at lighting speed. "I…" I started, but my voice trailed off, because the room started spinning, and my stomach ached in all the ways a stomach could ache. "I need air," I said, shoving past Victor and Nova and making a mad dash for the back door, not quite sure where it would lead me but knowing that if it was anywhere but here, there was a glimmer of hope that I might just be okay.

* * *

THE BACK DOOR led to a tiny and lightless alley. It was one that on any other given day, I would never even have considered visiting while solo, but on that night, in that moment, I found it overwhelmingly comforting. I leaned against the brick wall, in the darkness of the night, staring up at the moon, wondering where exactly I went wrong. Instantly, I decided that my greatest mistake had been permitting Victor Diaz to be a part of my life. Another part of me, the subliminal piece that wasn't yet doused in tequila, was screaming that this wasn't my fault. That we couldn't control who we fell in love with and not to be so hard on myself because there was *no* way I could have predicted this. There was *no* way he didn't care about me too. The evidence had been there all along, hadn't it?

I allowed my body to slide down the wall of the building behind me, the coolness of its surface providing an unexpected sense of comfort. I pressed my hands against my stomach in an effort to calm my nerves, but when that didn't work, I reached for my phone. I opened my Spotify app and located the first song I could think of, "Somewhere in Between" by Lifehouse. It was the only song on the face of the earth that could validate what I was going through, because I was without a doubt hanging on to something—everything—and I had no idea what was real and what was not.

"Summer? What the hell? Are you okay?"

I knew it was Victor, and I knew he was towering over me, but something within my entire being refused to look up at him. I focused intently on the phone in my hands, staring at the song lyrics as they flashed on the bottom of my screen. Some of them were beginning to blur, while others were legible. Victor didn't get me, but Lifehouse did. I could tell, based on the gut-wrenching song lyrics, that Lifehouse had had their hearts stomped on, just as Victor had done to me. Victor couldn't save me now. Victor wouldn't be the one to make me feel better, but music sure as hell would. I closed my eyes and anchored my head back against the building. "Is this real or just a dream?" I whispered, staring past Victor into the emptiness of the alley.

"Summer, stand up. Come on!"

But I had no intention of standing up. It was clear to me that I had fallen head over heels in love with someone who would never love me in the same way. Did he have any idea how that felt? To know with one hundred percent of my soul that I had found the love of my life but that I could never be his was confusing, excruciatingly painful, and honestly, really embarrassing. I could count dozens of times that his words, his touch, his promises were those of someone who was *way* more than a friend. But how could I have been so wrong about something I thought was so right?

"Victor," I whispered, suddenly caught off guard because the tiny alley I was resting in began to close in around us. "Victor," I said again, realizing then that he had extended his hand to me, and I was holding on to it for dear life. I opened my eyes and gazed up at him through the spinning, through all the spinning. "Victor?"

"Stand up, Summer. Come on!" he demanded, pulling me to my feet.

"Can someone be the worst and best thing that's ever happened to you?"

"What?" he asked, clearly confused. Victor wrapped his hands around my waist, pulling me close to him. "Please stop this," he whispered. "Not here."

"I said"—pausing for a beat and pointing my finger in his face, poking him on the nose by mistake—"can someone be the worst and best thing to ever happen to you?"

"Come on, Summer. I need to get you home."

"Because, Victor, you are the *best* thing to happen to me, but you are also the *worst*."

He hesitated, allowing me to lean my head back against the wall. I shut my eyes and took in the smell of him, all of him. The tequila on his breath, the musky scent of his cologne. They were scents I once found comforting, but now... now they were my enemies. I couldn't have him. I would never have him. I would never be his, and he would never be mine. His heart would always belong to her, and I would always be the sister, the friend.

"Why would you say that?" he asked, his words coming out in a choked sadness that I didn't recognize, and this snapped my eyes open, forcing me to shove my hands over my eyes. I hadn't wanted to make him sad.

"Can you... Can you stop pretending?" I begged more than asked.

"Pretending? Summer, what—"

I pressed my fingers to his lips to silence him. "It's obvious that I care more. It's getting a little embarrassing."

Victor removed my fingers from his lips. "What are you talking about?"

"Victor," I said, wrapping my hands behind his head and pulling his face closer to mine.

"Summer, please," he whispered. "I said not here."

"I think I love you."

Victor stopped breathing at this point. The beating of his heart increased against my chest, and the beads of sweat that were forming on his forehead permeated onto mine. I placed my hands on either side of his cheeks and pressed my nose against his.

"You think? Or you know?" he asked, his words coming out like a plea.

"I know." I pressed my lips against his, and although it was the first kiss we had ever shared, it felt like the thousandth. My body collapsed in his embrace as the softness of his lips pressed against mine, and for the first time in my life, I understood what it meant to be fully connected to another person. My tongue found his, and he grabbed the back of my neck, holding me down with just enough force and sweeping his tongue over my teeth and back around my mouth like we had done this a dozen times before. But just as the sadness began to dissipate from my soul and Lifehouse stopped playing from my phone, Victor pulled back.

"Summer, we can't—"

"I know."

"It will never—"

"I know, but what do I do now? I love you, and I can't make it stop." I pulled him close to me and kissed him again.

"Summer—" Victor started, but his words were cut short because someone burst through the back door of the building, made some sort of weird shrieking sound, flashed a light of some kind, and bolted away. "Shit!" Victor yelled into the darkness. "Shit, Summer, this is bad. Do you know how bad this is?"

I wasn't sure where it came from, but a deep laugh escaped from somewhere inside of me. "So bad," I said between drunken laughs.

"Victor?"

I turned to see Nova at the door, her long arms crossed over her shiny dress. It was then I realized that my fingers were still on Victor's face and his arms around my waist.

"You and Summer? Seriously?" Her mouth gaped open in shock as she stared at us in disbelief.

"Nova, it's not what it looks like," Victor said, holding his hands up and backing away.

"It's not?" I asked, my tone bolder than I intended. Maybe if it weren't for the four margaritas I had consumed in under an hour, I would have noticed the crowd of people gathering behind a completely pissed-off Nova. Maybe if I hadn't been completely intoxicated, devastated, rejected, and lonely, I would have made a better decision. But instead of walking away and assuring Nova and the crowd of spectators that this was not what it looked like, I took it upon myself to argue. "It *is* what it looks like. And I don't care who knows."

"Summer! Summer, stop!" he begged. "It's not going to happen. It's *never* going to happen."

I stared at him, wide-eyed. "You don't mean that."

"I do," he said, glancing over his shoulder at the sudden mob that formed outside the party. "I don't love you. I love Nova. It's *never* going to happen, Summer. I'm sorry if I did anything to make you think otherwise. It's never going to happen. You and me, Summer. It will *never* be a thing."

"Victor," I said, ignoring the uninvited tears starting to stream down my cheeks. "You're fired."

"No," he said, his voice trembling and his breath unsteady. "I quit."

PART THREE

JULY TWENTY-SECOND

TWO WEEKS LATER

CHAPTER FOURTEEN

JULY 22, 2002

MILLIE BIRD-JENNINGS

It was our first July at the Anderson cottage without Lark. She'd recently enlisted in the United States Coast Guard, and we couldn't have been prouder. On that week, Summer was thirteen, and my grandson, Blake, was seven years old. Blake, who had asked for a hamster every year on his birthday since he was two, was sitting on the living room floor, holding Hampton the hamster in his tiny hands while telling him knock-knock jokes, one of his favorite things to do. I sat in my favorite wicker rocking chair, rocking on the porch, admiring the waves of high tide as they crashed on shore and listening to Summer as she sat cross-legged on the porch step, strumming her guitar.

"Sounds beautiful," I told her, and I meant it.

"Thanks, Birdie," she said while continuing to play.

She smiled at me, and my heart burst with happiness. Summer had come so far in so many ways, and I couldn't help but feel that Al and I had played a huge part in her success. School wasn't too much of an issue for her anymore. She struggled here and there but nothing like when she was younger. She had friends at school, friends who shared interests like hers. It filled my heart with such joy that even though she was making friends and finding her place in life, she still found solace here, at the Anderson cottage, with her grandparents.

"Tell me the story of how you met Grandpa," she said through her sweet smile.

"Oh, girl, I've told you that story hundreds of times."

"But I love hearing it. And you *love* to tell it."

"I can't argue with that," I said with a nod. "It was a late-July evening in 1959. Our friend Art Young was throwing a party right here at the Anderson cottage, downstairs on the first floor."

"The men were playing poker."

"That's correct. The men were playing cards and smoking cigars. The women were standing by and watching."

"Why were they not playing?"

"It was different then. Then, men played cards, and the women watched. Sometimes, we served drinks."

"What was Grandpa drinking?"

"Old-fashioneds," I said with a smile.

"With extra cherries."

"Good girl, you remembered! Grandpa Al was drinking old-fashioneds with extra cherries, but I wasn't sitting with him. I was across the table with his good friend Philip."

"Your *boyfriend.*"

"Yes, that's right. I was going steady with Philip. And Philip wasn't the nicest guy. I liked him enough, but I knew he wasn't the one."

"Wait," Summer said, placing her guitar down next to me. "This is the first time you've said that."

"Said what?" I asked before sipping my coffee.

"That Philip wasn't the one."

"Well," I said, "I guess you're right. Philip wasn't the one.

He was a lot of fun to be around. He was handsome, he was smart, and he had a lot of friends. Looking back, I might say that I didn't so much like Philip as much as I liked how Philip made me feel."

"So, he was the popular guy."

"Yes."

"But he wasn't the one."

"Nope."

"And Grandpa Al?"

"Grandpa Al was quiet. Until that night, I hadn't said much to him."

"Until he won you in a game of poker," Summer said, pumping her fist in the air. "Grandpa Al for the win!"

I closed my eyes for a beat, remembering that moment as if it had happened five minutes ago. Al was seated across the table, straight-faced and serious. He always had an air of mystery about him. I was perched on Philip's lap, holding his cigar between my fingers while he placed his bet. He had been frustrated at that point and had lost all the money he came to play with. He must have thought he had a winning hand because instead of throwing in the towel, he threw his car keys in the center of the table.

When Al and Art argued that he was acting crazy, Philip said, "Oh yeah? Fine! Forget the car. I'll throw in Millie."

"Your grandfather's face was priceless," I told Summer. "Philip assumed that he wouldn't hold him to his end of the bargain, but oh, did he ever."

"You left the party with him that night."

"I sure did."

"And you kissed in his car at the Nubble."

"We sure did."

"And you lived happily ever after," Summer said, climbing onto my lap.

"Amen, girl." I kissed her forehead, thankful that even

though she was growing like a weed and turning into a teenager before my very eyes, she still loved to snuggle with me.

"What's going on out here?" Al asked, rounding the corner.

"I made Birdie tell me the story of how you first met."

"Again?"

"Yes," I said. "But I didn't mind."

"That was a good night. That moron, Philip, gave me the best thing that ever happened to me," Al said before kissing the top of my head.

"Gross." Summer giggled. "I'm going to play with Blake and Hampton."

"Make sure you lock that cage tight," I reminded her, as Hampton had gone loose twice that summer and ended up downstairs with Sean and Gerry.

"Yes, Birdie," she said before hopping down and heading inside.

Al sat down next to me in his rocking chair and took my hand in his. "That was the best night of my life," he said, bringing my fingers to his mouth for a kiss.

"And mine."

"I love you, Birdie. I always have, and I always will."

"I know," I said with a wink. "I love you too."

CHAPTER FIFTEEN

JULY 22, 2023

SUMMER ROSE JENNINGS

*I*t has been a week since my night out for drinks with Thena, and we have since gotten together twice—once more for drinks and then again for breakfast with Oakley. I adore watching Thena with her daughter. She is so quick to anticipate Oakley's needs, knowing what she is going to ask for or want even before her daughter does. It was that morning, over eggs sunny-side up and a double side of bacon, that Thena broke the news. I was midsip of coffee when she peered up and me and said, "Oh, and on a side note, Brad said that this week works for you to come on set and meet Lawson Remington."

It took everything within me not to spit my coffee all over the table. Instead, I choked on it, taking a considerable amount of time to get my coughing under control. "I'm sorry. Did you just say I get to meet Lawson?"

"Yes!" she had squealed in delight. "As long as you can get the day off. He said Saturday would work because they're doing some outside shots right on Long Sands by the Anderson cottage."

"Thena, I love you!" I exclaimed, reaching over the table and wrapping my arms around her. "I'll get the day off."

I had driven to Kittery and hit up the outlets in an effort to locate the perfect outfit. But what does a person wear when they meet their lifelong celebrity crush? When they, too, are an actual celebrity? Back in LA, I had a stylist, and I very seldom needed to give my wardrobe a second thought. Since the meeting would be on the beach, I stuck with my favorite pair of denim cutoffs and a shirt I'd purchased from J. Crew, a flowy, beachy, white button-down blouse over a multicolored floral crop top. After blow-drying and straightening my hair for well over an hour and confirming that makeup was on point, I'd slid on my favorite pair of sandals, tossed my bag over my shoulder, and exited my motel room.

"Heading anywhere fun?"

I leap back in surprise, not expecting River to be leaning against the porch railing, sipping what looks to be a protein shake or a smoothie of some kind. He's wearing tan khaki shorts and an Army green fitted T-shirt he's matched with a Boston Celtics baseball cap and dark sunglasses. "Just another day," I say, not sure why I'm finding it necessary to lie to my neighbor about meeting Lawson. It is no secret that they are filming on Long Sands today. A large stretch of beach will be closed, and it is all I've heard anyone talk about over the past couple of days.

He tilts his head and raises an eyebrow. "Well, if it's just another day, you look really nice for someone who's going to be cleaning motel rooms."

I roll my eyes at him, annoyed with his comment. *Why would this guy be so curious about my plans for the day?* I think for a beat, moving closer to him and mimicking his stance, and then it hits me. He *knows* who I am. Last week, when we met in this very spot, he pretended like he didn't know who I was, but of course he knows. He knew about my brother, my parents, and my grandparents. How would he not know about me? "You know who I am, don't you?" I accuse, a bit sassier than I mean to.

He drops his sunglasses down, and I look up at him, studying him intently. "I don't know what you mean," he says with a shrug and a smirk. His serious dark eyes taunt me.

"I think you're full of crap," I challenge.

This makes him smile, and I sort of like it. He strikes me as the kind of person who doesn't typically waste too much time making small talk or playing around. "Okay, Summer Jennings, you're right. I know who you are."

"You do?"

He chews on the side of his straw and angles his head. "Yes, but don't worry. I won't tell anyone."

"Most people around here know." I sigh.

"Yeah, it must be really hard being an undercover agent for the FBI."

"What?" I blurt. I shove my hands on my hips and stare up at him, wide-eyed. "I am not an undercover agent for the FBI."

"I know." He chuckles, and I relax for a beat. "Because everyone knows you are an escaped convict from a maximum-security women's prison who was serving twenty years for a crime so disturbing I can't actually say it out loud."

Who the hell does this guy think he is? I reach up and pull the tip of his cap down playfully, finally realizing what he is doing. "I'm not an escaped convict," I say through my laughter. "Why are you doing this?"

"Doing what?"

"Acting like you don't know me."

"I don't know you."

"You know what I mean. You know *of* me."

"But I don't know you."

I shake my head and bite my lip, trying to figure him out.

"And I don't know you," I say, raising my eyebrows and pointing my finger at him. "Who are you, anyway?"

He slurps the remaining drink and places the plastic cup down on the railing. "I'm River Frost."

"I know your name. But who are you? Why are you living in a motel for the summer? And why do you care so much about who I am and what I'm doing today?" My words come out jumbled together, and by the time I'm done asking the questions, I am out of breath. Annoyed and out of breath.

He crosses his arms over his chest, and I can't help but move my eyes to his biceps. I can tell by their size and shape that River likes to work out. He also has a tattoo on his left arm, the one closest to me. It looks like multiple shapes in a cluster of some sort with something written in cursive, but the sun is bright, and I can't make it out. His silence becomes uncomfortable, and I am ready to tell him that I'm leaving now, that as soon as my ride gets here, I will be going to meet Lawson Remington. Then River takes in a deep breath, holds it for a second or two, and says, "Coffee."

"Coffee? What does that have to do with anything?"

"I want to take you to coffee."

"You want to take me, a girl you know nothing about, to coffee."

"How else will I get to know you?"

I think about this for a beat. "No."

"No?"

"No to coffee. Yes to drinks."

"Drinks?"

"Yes. Because I know you know who I am. And if I am going to have to relive my life's greatest failures, it's going to have to be over drinks."

"Drinks, it is."

"Tonight?" I ask, surprising myself. "I mean, if you're around. Considering I know nothing about you, you could be a serial killer for all I know. What time do serial killers start work? I'm assuming once it gets dark?"

"I should be off work tonight by sunset," he says.

"See," I say, nodding with satisfaction. "Serial killer… or a werewolf. Although you are kind of too cute to be a werewolf." My comment was meant to be funny, but the second I say it, I wish I could take it back.

"So tonight, then," he says, fighting back a smile. "Sea-Pub."

"Sounds good," I say, checking the time on my phone. My ride to the Anderson cottage should have been here by now, and I search the parking lot in confusion.

"Looking for someone?"

"Yeah, I am. My ride was supposed to be here by now."

"Oh, that's right, your ride. To the Anderson cottage. To meet Lawson?"

"How did you know—"

River dangles his keys inches from my face. "'Cause I'm your ride, Summer Jennings."

I shake my head and cover my face with my hands. "Of course you are."

"Come on. I've got the boss's Maserati."

"What, are you an actor or something? A director?"

"Worse, a PA. Come on. Let's go." River hops the railing and makes his way to a shiny black sports car, and for the first time in over a week, my heart feels something that sort of resembles joy.

THE RIDE from the Seabird Motel to the Anderson cottage was roughly ten minutes due to traffic. I would have walked there myself, but I needed River to gain access to the cottage, as a large radius had been blocked off for today's filming. I was surprisingly quiet on the ride, sneaking discreet side glances at Riv, a tad curious about him and his work on the movie set.

"You doing okay?" he asked as we pulled up to the back of the Anderson cottage.

"I'm a bit nervous," I admitted. "Nervous and excited."

"I know someone back home who calls that nervous-ited."

I laughed, resisting the urge to follow up his statement with a dozen questions. Where was back home? *Who* was back home? But I decided to save my questions for tonight. I had been too busy fighting off the millions of butterflies that fluttered throughout my stomach because I was going to be meeting Lawson Remington, a man I had been crushing on since I was a preteen, and I had so many emotions I didn't know where to begin.

Now, as River and I walk barefoot in the sands of Long Sands Beach and the Anderson cottage comes into focus, the butterflies turn to nausea, and my knees grow weak. I stop for a moment and place my hands on my belly.

"You good?" he asks.

"Of course," I say, a bit embarrassed. "I've just been waiting for this for a really long time."

"He's just a normal guy," River reassures me.

But could that be my problem? For years, I have crushed on this guy, and maybe some of my anxiety is stemming from the possibility that I might not even like him as a person.

"I know," I say confidently. "Thank you."

"Here we are," River says as we approach a sectioned-off area of the beach, directly adjacent from the three-story gray cottage. "You ready?"

"Ready as I'll ever be."

River leads me over to a space with chairs, tables,

cameras, monitors, and various types of sound and recording equipment. This was not a new scene for me, as I have filmed multiple music videos in the past and filmed a handful of commercials. But being here, on this movie set, in my hometown, with my celebrity crush, fills me with so much excitement that I can't put it into words. River grabs a walkie-talkie from the table and says something into it that I don't quite make out. He throws his head back in frustration and sighs. He says something else, nods his head, and continues talking. I must make a nervous face of some kind because he winks at me reassuringly, and I relax a bit. River walks in my direction and points at the cottage. "So, here's the thing. Lawson is inside the Anderson cottage, and he doesn't want to come out until filming starts."

"Oh," I say, my disappointment not going unnoticed.

"But we can go inside, and you can meet him there. I just need you to sign a few documents. It's nothing, really, just some privacy stuff."

"Oh," I say, breathing a sigh of relief. "That's no big deal at all."

"Come on," he says with confidence. "Let's head inside, and we can take it from there."

I follow him up the hill to the cottage, struggling at times to keep up with his long and energetic strides. "So, he's living here, then? That's interesting."

"Yes. He thought by staying at the cottage, it would help him get into character."

"I can see that."

"That's why the nondisclosure clause is so important. If word gets out that he is living here…"

"Say no more. I totally understand. I know a thing or two about the importance of privacy."

"I'm sure you do," he says seriously. "Being a professional waterslide tester must really be tough—"

"A professional waterslide tester? Really?"

"Sorry, I forgot. Being a professional bridesmaid must really be tough."

"I've decided that I'm going to start ignoring you."

"Or you can just admit what you really do."

"I'm not doing that."

"Why?"

"Because you already know what I do. That's why." We start our hike up the stairs of the cottage. We continue past the second floor, so I assume Lawson is staying on the third. "Are Sean and Cassidy staying here throughout the filming?"

"Nah, they're renting a place in York Harbor. The chaos is a bit much with the new baby and all."

"That's right," I say, remembering now that I'd recently seen a picture of their new little family on Instagram, including the tiniest little redheaded baby girl named Josephine. "I don't blame them for not sticking around. This place sure isn't as quiet as it usually is."

"You've stayed here before?" he asks, knocking on the sliding door.

"Yes," I say, tracing my fingers over the white wicker rocking chair and gazing out at low tide. A breeze meets my face, and I turn my attention to the wide patches of seagrass and weeds in the distance. "The seagrass is dancing," I say under my breath, remembering a moment I shared with my grandparents.

My thoughts come to a complete halt as the slider is pulled open with one strong thrust, and there standing between me and a place that holds more childhood memories than I can count is Lawson Remington.

"Summer Jennings," he says, his voice deeper than I expected it to be. "Look what the cat dragged in."

River pats Lawson on the shoulder of his white T-shirt. "Lawson, this is Summer. Summer, this is Lawson," River says, pointing to me and back to Lawson and back to me again. Lawson looks like I thought he would, but he is shorter than I imagined, which is what people always say to me upon meeting me too. Cameras are funny like that. There is no way of telling how tall a person is just by watching them on screen.

He runs a hand through his shaggy brown hair and extends his hand out for a handshake. "Sean," he states with confidence. "Sean Anderson."

I furrow my brow in confusion and reach for his hand. "Summer Jennings," I say, not sure if using my real name suits this moment.

"I'm just playing." Lawson laughs. "But seriously, how did I do? I've been working on that for months now."

"You did great."

"That's cool of you to say," he says.

"Can we come in or what, man?" Riv asks, checking his Apple watch for the time. "We've got to stay on schedule today."

Lawson moves to the side and gestures for us to come in. I am instantly disappointed that the third floor has been renovated. It looks gorgeous, but I had been hoping for the same tiny kitchen table that I sat at with Birdie and Al as I ate my Fruity Pebbles, but my disappointment disappears quickly because I am standing in the kitchen of the Anderson cottage and across from Lawson Remington. I wrack my brain to come up with something, anything to ask Lawson, but suddenly, I have forgotten how to speak.

"So, how do you like York?" Lawson asks.

"Me? Oh, I sort of grew up here."

"No kidding. Right here on Long Sands?"

"Well, yeah," I say with a smile. "But when I say I grew up here, I mean, like, I grew up *here*." I extend my arms out in reference to the living room and kitchen of the cottage.

"No way," he says. "You grew up at this cottage?"

"Yes," I said. "Some of my happiest memories were here. With my grandparents."

"Did you know Sean and Cassidy, then?"

"Well, I knew Sean. We grew up together. He was closer in age to my sister Lark—"

"Wait a second. You're telling me that you lived here in this cottage and that you know Sean."

"Yes."

"Hey, Riv, how long do I have until we shoot?"

"Four minutes and twenty-five seconds."

"Well, that's not enough time at all," he says, stepping closer to me and placing his hand on my shoulder. "I need to know everything you know about this cottage and Sean Anderson."

I'm dead. I've died and gone to Heaven. That is the only logical explanation for this scenario. Lawson's hand is on my shoulder. Lawson wants to spend more time with *me.* I turn and face River, who wears a stone-cold expression. I look from him to Lawson. I can't believe I am standing this close to him. "What do you need to know?" I ask, my voice a shaky mess.

"Everything," he says with a smile. "Over drinks."

"Drinks?" I ask, my eyes bulging out of my face. *Stop fangirling him, Summer!* I beg myself. But it's hopeless. Lawson's hand is rubbing my arm, and his wide, toothy smile has taken over my soul.

"Yeah, drinks. Just stay and hang out for the filming and then come back up. I've got a few bottles of wine in the fridge, and the team will hook us with some grub. You can grab dinner, can't you, Riv?"

Riv's cheeks flush a deep sunburn red, and his jaw tightens. "Of course, man. Just let me know what you want."

Lawson brushes a strand of hair behind my ear, and my heart stops. "Did you have plans tonight, Summer Jennings?"

Plans? Tonight? My mind has drawn a blank, like the people in that movie *Men in Black* when their memories were wiped clean by that weird-looking pen thingy. "Me? Gosh no. I've got absolutely nothing going on. I'll be here."

CHAPTER SIXTEEN

JULY 22, 2023

RIVER FROST

I am sitting on a bench at the Nubble Lighthouse, overlooking the waves as they crash against the rocky shore. We wrapped up filming earlier than expected, which is always a good thing. So why, then, do I have this feeling of dread in the pit of my stomach? It began when I pulled away from the cottage, knowing damn well that I was leaving Summer with a complete asshole. Of course, Summer is an adult. But she hadn't gotten to know Lawson in the same way I had. The dude has had a different girl in his bed every night since we began filming. To Summer, Lawson is a god. To Lawson, Summer is simply another celebrity that he's going to add to his résumé.

I reach for my phone because Kinsley is supposed to be FaceTiming me. I told her about the sunsets at the Nubble Lighthouse, and I made a promise to her that if it worked out for both of our schedules, I would FaceTime her during the sunset. I glance up at the clear sky and study it as it changes from crystal-clear blue to slight shades of pink and purple. I send her a text to remind her that filming ended early and since my plans have changed, she can call me, and we can watch the sunset. My text doesn't receive a response, but my phone begins to ring with a FaceTime call from Kinsley. My heart bursts with joy as I swipe open the screen, and there staring back at me is my blond-haired, blue-eyed Kinsley. My twelve-year-old baby girl.

"Hey, Dad!" she shrieks with happiness. "Are you there? Are you at that lighthouse?"

"I am, darling! I'm here. I told the sunset to wait for you, and it listened to me."

"Really?"

"Really."

"Show me!"

I switch the screen so she can see what I see. The multi-colored sky, the setting sun, and the crashing waves. "Can you see it?" I ask.

"Yes, I see it. It's so pretty, Daddy. Show me the lighthouse. The one from the books."

I steady my phone and move it slowly so that she can take in the tiny but mighty Nubble Lighthouse as it stands strong on its hill overlooking the Atlantic. "It's starting to get dark. Can you see the lighthouse?"

"Yes! Thank you!"

I flip the screen so it is focused back on me. I study her for a beat and wish I could reach through the screen and kiss her cheeks. "I miss you, baby," I say, forcing a smile but wiping away a single tear that I've allowed to escape from my eye.

"I miss you too."

"How was camp?"

"Great! I passed the swim test, and I got a lead in the play."

"That's my girl!" I yell, pumping my fist in the air. A few people around me turn and stare, but I don't care. "What part did you get?"

"I got the role of Elle Woods in *Legally Blonde*."

"Get out! Really?"

"Really."

"I'm not surprised," I say. "You're a very talented girl. When is the play?" I ask, knowing that more than likely, I'm not going to be able to be there, which saddens me in a way I can't even begin to fathom.

"It's on a Friday night. August fourth, I think."

"What time?"

"Mom! What time is my play?"

I hear Sarah in the background, but I can't make out what she is saying. If it's after seven o'clock, then there is the slightest chance I could make it to the play.

"It's at five p.m.," Kinsley says, locking eyes with mine over FaceTime. "Will you be there?"

My heart sinks. August 4 is a huge previously scheduled production date. There is no way I would be able to get back into the city by five thirty on that day and keep my job. But her eyes are pleading, and her smile is wide, and for some reason unbeknownst to me, I find myself agreeing to August 4 at five thirty. Kinsley cheers and tells me she loves me. We hang up, and I hold the phone close to my chest as if somehow, it keeps her with me for a moment longer. Not even a second goes by before I get a text, and I don't even have to look at it to know it is Sarah, but I do anyway.

> Sarah: What are you thinking? Promising her you will be there? Come on, River. Really?

> River: If I say I'll be there, then I'll be there, Sarah. Cut me some slack.

She responds, but I'm too angry to read it in this moment. I've learned when it comes to Sarah that sometimes, I simply need to give her time and space. If I can give her those two things, she usually comes around.

Sarah and I met in film school out in Cali. We fell in love junior year and were inseparable after that. After graduation, we both got our feet wet in the industry in different ways, but our schedules were both demanding, to say the least. We were married in 2008 and had Kinsley in 2009. Everything was going better than I could have imagined until Sarah took a job as a PA on a movie set out in LA and slept with the producer, getting pregnant with his son. As if that weren't bad enough, the producer was married and begged Sarah to keep their relationship a secret. One stupid decision left Sarah pregnant by a man who didn't want to father her child and with a husband who could no longer trust her.

We tried to make it work. Really, we did. But in the end, Sarah was going to have another baby, and I couldn't trust Sarah. She told me one day over text that she would be leaving California to live with her mother in Boston, and she wanted to take Kinsley with her. The courts ruled for shared custody, and because I believed that being in Boston would be what was best for Kinsley, I agreed to move too. Which is how I ended up here, at the Nubble Lighthouse in York, Maine, filming a movie starring one of Hollywood's greatest assholes who is now at the Anderson cottage, hitting on the first girl I have had feelings for in over ten years.

I stand up and tuck my phone away in my pocket. Part of me wants to drive back to the Anderson cottage and pick Summer up, but another piece of me, the one who understands she is not a child, knows that she can make her own decisions and date who she wants to date. Instead, I decide to head back to the Seabird and call it an early night. I'm not entirely sure how I am going to make it to Kinsley's play on August 4, but I know that I'm going to try harder than anything I've ever done before to make it there.

CHAPTER SEVENTEEN

JULY 22, 2023

SUMMER ROSE JENNINGS

I'm on my third glass of wine when I realize that Lawson Remington is a complete asshole. So far, in the past three hours, he has talked about himself, Sean Anderson, himself, and—let me think—himself. I've gone from disappointed to annoyed, frustrated, and even more disappointed. We are seated on the sofa in the living room of the Anderson cottage's third floor, talking about how he landed the role of Sean Anderson and how much it means to him.

His words become background noise as I study the living room. I remember my time with Birdie and my grandfather like it was yesterday—the trips to the arcade, playing the guitar with Birdie. My unhappiness with Lawson has little to do with the fact he has disappointed me greatly and more to do with the idea that he might be taking away from my memories here, in this space, and those memories are more precious to me than some actor who thinks he's getting laid tonight.

As if on cue, Lawson places his hand on my knee. "So

how about you, Summer? Did you really sleep with your manager?"

He leans forward, and I think he is going to kiss me, but instead, he places his hand on my boob and moves the other one up my thigh.

"No," I say, moving his hands off me. "I didn't sleep with my manager."

Lawson is either oblivious to my discomfort, or he really doesn't care. "That's not what I read," he says, sliding his hand up my leg and between my thighs.

I grab his hand again and shove it away from me in one sweep. "Please," I say, the blood rushing to my cheeks. I gather my hair over my shoulder and bite my lower lip. I stare down at the ground, afraid of looking up at him. "I… uh… I need to use the restroom," I say, hopping to my feet.

"It's down the hall—"

"I know where it is." I stand and make my way down the hallway and lock the bathroom door behind me. *What is wrong with me?* Wouldn't any girl in my position be jumping at the opportunity to be with Lawson Remington? Hadn't I fantasized about this for my entire life? Hadn't I wondered what it would be like to kiss him? To touch him? Why does this feel so wrong? Is it because of Victor? Did I mess myself up so badly with Victor that I will never be able to open myself up again with anyone? Even Lawson? I don't have the answers to these questions. I don't know what I want. But I do know what I don't want, and I don't want to have casual sex with Lawson Remington.

I pull out my phone and lean my head against the bathroom door. I consider texting Blake, but I'm still mad at him for telling me I could come home and then making me clean motel rooms. I could text Thena, but she is most likely busy with Oakley, and I can't do that to her at this hour. Which leaves… River.

I've never been so thankful for anyone in this moment, as he took my phone from me prior to his departure and added his number in my contacts, probably because he knows what a jerk Lawson is and anticipated my needing a ride home. I mean, I could totally walk, but being alone right now would be like pouring salt in an open wound, because even though I am completely and utterly disappointed that Lawson turned out to be sort of a loser, I'm finding myself thinking of Victor again, and that is just a recipe for disaster. I take a deep breath and locate River in my contacts, laughing out loud when I realize he saved his name in my contacts as River Frost PA, and in the notes section of my contacts, he has written, *Call me when you realize what a scumbag Lawson is and you need me to come get you.* I stifle back a laugh as I type.

Summer: Hi

River Frost PA: Hi

Summer: So, I…

River Frost PA: I'll be there in five.

I sigh with relief, use the bathroom, wash my hands, and head back toward the living room, but Lawson is no longer seated on the couch. "Hello?" I call into the empty room. "Lawson?"

I peek my head outside onto the porch, but he isn't outside. I consider bolting from the cottage and walking down the street until River sees me and picks me up, but I have always been in love with Lawson—or the idea of him—and bailing on him just seems like such a letdown. I need to say goodbye and thank him for taking the time to meet me. So I head back inside, but when I reach the living room, I hear him call my name from the bedroom.

"I'm in here," he calls out.

"I, um, I…" I start, but my voice trails off, because as I round the corner to what used to be my grandparents' bedroom, I find Lawson—naked. He is leaning against the bedroom door with a look in his eyes like he wants to eat me alive. I steady my eyes on his, my expression serious as I fix my gaze on his face. "I'm leaving. Thank you very much for having me."

"What?" he asks, raising his eyebrows, his eyes growing wide. "Is this some kind of joke?"

"Why would this be a joke?"

"Because isn't this what you wanted?"

I cringe because he is right. Once upon a time, this is what I wanted. There was a time in my life where being with Lawson would have been a dream come true. But I'm not the same girl I used to be. And the person I am trying to become makes better choices than this. Lawson Remington or not, I'm going to be better. I'm going to *do* better. "How would you know what I want, Lawson? You don't know me." I turn from him and make my way down the hallway and out of the cottage. I can hear him yelling something in the distance, but I don't stick around to find out what. I bolt down the stairs, hopeful that River is waiting out back for me, and he is. I've never been so thankful to see anyone in my entire life. I get in the car, slam the door, and bury my face in my hands.

River puts the car in reverse, and as I stare out the window into the darkness of the night, I study the stars. I vaguely remember something Blake said to me about counting the stars, on the night I called him from LA, so I try to count them, hopeful that this strategy might keep me from bursting into tears in front of River. But I can't count the stars. All I seem to be able to do is count my regrets. I regret auditioning for *Rise 2 Fame*. I regret meeting Victor Diaz. I regret my obsession with Lawson Remington. And I regret blowing River off for drinks. Sweet, sexy, and cute River, who dropped whatever he was doing to come get me and who anticipated that I would need him even before I did. Sort of like how Thena knows what Oakley needs before she even consciously knows it.

"I'm sorry I blew you off tonight," I whisper to the window, more to him.

"It's okay," he says gently. "I totally get it."

"You do?" I ask, finally turning my head and looking at him. He wears a backward baseball cap, gym shorts, and a gray hoodie. I like this look on him a lot.

"Of course I do. I mean, what you do for a living is extremely dangerous."

My lips curl into a half smile, and without giving it a second thought, I lean my head on his shoulder and curl up against his arm. I don't know him well at all. But I know myself. And I need his comfort like I need air. "It is?"

"Well, yeah, Summer. Not everyone can pull off being a snake milker."

I choke on my laugh and bury my face in the sleeve of his sweatshirt. "What in the actual hell is a snake milker?"

"Look it up," he says with a smirk, interlacing his fingers in mine.

"Thank you," I whisper so softly that I'm not sure if he's even heard me.

"For what?"

"For being there. It just… it feels so nice to know I'm not alone."

* * *

I AM SCOOPING up my dirty laundry and hiding it under my bed when Riv returns from his motel room with two Corona Lights. We had decided on the ride home that if we had a couple of beers in my room that technically I didn't blow him off, and I wouldn't have to lie awake all night thinking about what a complete jerk I had been.

"Wow, that's quite the beauty," River exclaims.

I stare at him wide-eyed, wondering if he is referring to me and, if so, a little caught off guard.

"The guitar," he says with a laugh. "Man, what did you think I meant?"

"Oh," I said, sitting cross-legged on my bed and reaching for my guitar.

River sits next to me on the edge of the bed and traces his fingers over the body of the guitar.

I blush, finding the way he traces it so gently a turn-on. "You play?" I ask.

"I dabble," he says with a smile.

I nod, knowing very well that a person who says they play a little or they dabble is code for "I'm freaking amazing."

I take a swig of my beer and place it on the nightstand. "Play me something."

"Now?"

"Yes, now."

He sips his beer and places it on the opposing nightstand. "What do you want to hear?"

"Know any songs about girls who blow up their careers and almost sleep with their celebrity crushes who turn out to be total losers?"

"No," he says, looking amused. "But I do know one that you might like."

I lean back against the bed's headboard and bring my knees to my chest. A breeze comes through my window, sending a chill over my bare legs. "Wait," I say, holding a finger up. "I need to get a sweatshirt."

"Don't get up," he says, laying the guitar between us. He lifts his hoodie over his head and tosses it my way.

His T-shirt has lifted a bit, revealing his abdomen, and I

look away quickly, embarrassed for staring. He pulls his shirt down and reaches for my guitar. I shimmy the hoodie over my head and allow the warmth from his body heat to comfort me in a way that I am unfamiliar with. It also smells like him, smoky and spicy, which is another pleasant surprise. I decide in this moment that he might never get this sweatshirt back.

"Where did you get the guitar?" he asks.

"Oh, I didn't *get* it. It's my grandmother's. It's been in my family forever. It's the only acoustic I've ever played."

"It's beautiful." He's talking about my guitar, but he's looking at me.

"I just love music. It's the only thing I've ever really been able to connect with."

"How so?"

"When I was really little, I stopped talking."

"Like, completely?"

"I mean, for the most part, yes. I wouldn't talk at school. The only time I would talk to anyone was at the Anderson cottage with Birdie."

"Wow. I had no idea."

"I don't talk about it much. I didn't bring it up on *Rise 2 Fame* because I didn't want to be the contestant with the sob story." I pull his sweatshirt over my knees and hug them close, loving how his hoodie is big enough to fit all of me. "The teachers would let me listen to the radio because it was the only thing that eased my anxieties. Even to this day, I don't do great talking about my emotions. Instead, I name songs that describe how I'm feeling."

"I can totally relate to that," he says, allowing his fingers to pluck the guitar strings. I am instantly mesmerized at how easily they move over each string, effortlessly and so gracefully.

"My friend and I do this thing," I say, surprising myself

for sharing this. "Instead of texting how are you, or is everything okay, she will ask me, what's on your playlist? And I name a song and an artist, and she instantly knows how I'm feeling and how she can help."

"That's really cool," he says as he starts to strum the guitar to a melody I've never heard before. "What's on your playlist now, Summer Jennings?"

I blush, surprised that he's put me on the spot. "Right now, right now?"

"Yes, right now."

"I thought you were going to play me a song."

"I will, but first I want to know what's on your playlist."

I stare up at the ceiling and contemplate his question for a moment. "Snow Patrol is the artist."

"Song?"

"'Chasing Cars.'"

"Damn, that's a good one. What about that song qualifies it as the one on your list right now?"

I scoot down on the bed and lie on my side, pulling the hood of his sweatshirt over my head and resting on my elbow. "It talks about lying here and just forgetting the world. That's how I feel right now, in this moment, with you."

If my response shakes him in any way, he doesn't falter. He continues strumming my guitar with that serious and mysterious look that he makes and nods. "Good answer."

"It's the truth. So, are you playing me a song, or what?"

"I don't know, Summer. I wouldn't want to wake your neighbor," he says seriously.

I grab a pillow and throw it at him. "You're the neighbor."

"I know."

"So, play me something. Please?"

He adjusts his backward cap, closes his eyes, and begins to strum a melody that I know like the back of my hand—

because I wrote it. River Frost is sitting on my bed, playing my guitar, and it's a song I wrote. I rest my head on my arm and stare at him, unable to remove my eyes from this completely handsome man as he feels every beat and every note to *my* song. My heart starts beating faster, and chills run up and down my spine. And just when I think I can't take any more of this, River begins to sing. The air catches in the back of my throat, and I gasp. His voice is perfect—deep and raspy but sexy all at the same time. Like a combination of Isaac Slade of the Fray and Dave Matthews with a touch of Eddie Vedder of Pearl Jam.

He finishes the first two verses of my song, and by the time he is singing the chorus, I'm smitten. "When I'm with you, I see the bluest skies. When I'm with you, you give me butterflies. So safe in your arms, nothing to hide, you've kissed away all the tears I've cried." His eyes remain closed, and I'm thankful for this because I'm crying and probably drooling, and I can't take much more of this.

He finishes playing the last note. It is supposed to be an A, but he plays an E, but I am so incredibly distracted by the way his eyes glow from the light of the moon that for the first time in my life, I could care less about a musical note. Instead, I pull myself up to a seated position and carefully remove my guitar from his grip and lean it against the wall.

He remains seated on the corner of my bed, one foot crossed over his opposing knee, and my focus lands on his black Converse sneakers. I wipe my tears with the sweatshirt's sleeve, and I suddenly feel way too vulnerable, and I need to change the subject and fill this awkward silence. "My mom worked for Converse for years."

"You don't say?"

"I do say. I bet I can get you a pair at a discounted rate. She still has connections."

"I would love that."

"You know my music," I say, pointing at my guitar. "Like, you *really* know my music."

"Yup."

"So, what, you're a superfan?"

"I'm a fan," he says, choosing his words carefully. "Someone really special to me back home asked me to learn it for them."

"Oh," I say, suddenly disappointed. Of course there was someone back home. How could I be so stupid as to assume he was single? "So, you have a girlfriend, then? A wife?"

"No." He laughs. "Nothing like that."

"Oh."

"A story for another day?" he asks, his eyes pleading like they are saying I have so much to tell you but this night has been perfect, so please stop asking questions. "When we go out for real, I'll tell you about my past, and you tell me what happened out in LA. Deal?"

"Deal."

"It's getting late. I think I'm going to head home. It's a long drive," he says with a wink.

Disappointment washes over me, and I am instantly shocked at how badly I don't want him to leave. But he's right. It's been a long day and an even longer night.

River stands from my bed, picks up his beer, and takes one last swig. "Are you working tomorrow?" he asks.

"Thanks to my evil baby brother, yes."

River raises his eyebrows and pauses for a beat, like he is considering saying something about this but decides against it. "Well, that's good because my room is in desperate need of some good housekeeping, and I really like the way you fluff the pillows."

"Well, if you don't put the service sign on your door, then I won't know to go in there," I challenge.

"Point taken," he says, locking his eyes on mine. "Are you sure you're okay, Summer?"

I contemplate his question and decide that yes, I'm going to be okay. Even though my meet and greet with Lawson was a total failure, it feels nice to know that there is someone like River out there. Even if he has somebody back home, even if he isn't the one for me, it's nice to know that somewhere out there, there is a guy like him who could be the guy for me. "Yes," I say with confidence. "But can I please keep your hoodie? At least for tonight?"

River's lips curl into a smile, and he nods. "Yes, Summer, you can keep my hoodie. But I expect extra little bottles of shampoo tomorrow, or I'll be complaining to the management."

PART FOUR

JULY TWENTY-NINTH

ONE WEEK LATER

CHAPTER EIGHTEEN

JULY 29, 2002

MILLIE BIRD-JENNINGS

I was cleaning up after dinner when I heard Blake's ear-piercing screams. "Birdie! He's gone! Hampton! He's not in his cage!"

"I'm coming!" I had hollered down the hallway.

I handed Al the last dish, and he began to dry it.

"If we find that moron of a hamster"—he grunted—"I'm going to murder it myself. Why couldn't they have gotten the kid a puppy? Or a kitten, even? I'll never understand it."

I made my way down the hallway to find Blake on his hands and knees, looking under the bed for his pet. "He's gone," he wailed. "He ran away."

"He's got to be here somewhere," I reassured him. "Last time, he was downstairs with Sean and Gerry. Why don't we go see if that's where he went again?"

"Okay."

"Where's Summer?" I asked.

"I'm not sure. She was here a little while ago."

I took Blake by the hand, and we made our way down the stairs to the second floor of the Anderson cottage. I knocked on the slider, and Sean answered. I was hoping he might have looked better than he had the last time I saw him, but that wasn't the case. He clearly hadn't shaved in weeks, and the dark circles under his eyes were proof that he wasn't sleeping.

"Hampton ran away," Blake said with a pout.

Sean rubbed his face with his hands. "Again?"

"Yes," he said, wiping away his tears.

"Go on in," Sean said, gesturing to the inside of the cottage. "You can look. Just be quiet in the living room. My grandpa is sleeping in his armchair."

"Thank you," he said, scooting past Sean.

I studied him and decided that I didn't like what I saw. "Have you been eating?"

He shifted his gaze to the floor. "No, not really."

"You're worried about him?" I asked.

"It's bad," he said, referring to Gerry Anderson's Alzheimer's.

"What can we do?"

"There is really nothing anyone can do. I promised him no hospitals. I just don't know how much longer I can go on like this."

"Have you heard from that girl?"

Sean's jaw tightened, and he shook his head. "Cassidy? No. It was a summer fling."

"Yes, I know that. But she was so good with Gerry, wasn't she? He was quite fond of her."

"She's going to law school in Boston. We just grew apart. That's all."

The poor guy had heartbreak written all over his face. "You let me know what I can do."

"Thank you."

Blake exited the cottage with a frown. "I didn't find him."

"Let's go look upstairs again," I suggested. "Maybe he went home. Good night, Sean."

"Good night, Birdie."

"Hampton!" Blake called, running up the stairs ahead of me.

I followed closely behind, wondering how I would pick up the pieces of Blake and his broken heart if Hampton didn't make an appearance before bedtime. I entered the cottage and headed toward Blake's room, but I paused because I heard whispers coming from Blake's room. Curious as to what they might be up to, I leaned against the door and cupped my ear with my hand.

"I brought him back safe and sound, Blake. Please, Blake. Can't it be our secret?"

"But Summer! I was so worried."

"I know, and I'm sorry. I shouldn't have taken him without asking. You have every right to be mad at me. But *please* don't tell Birdie."

The idea that Summer had had something to do with Hampton's disappearance was mind-blowing to say the least. But knowing that Hampton was back at the Anderson cottage safe and sound was a huge relief.

"Okay, Summer. I won't."

"Do you promise? Promise me you won't tell her? I'll win you the bonus-ticket prize at the arcade tomorrow. Here, pinkie swear."

"I promise."

I knocked on the door, pretending that I wasn't aware of Hampton's return. "Did you find him?"

"Yes!" both kids shrieked at the same time.

I bent down over Hampton's cage and pressed my finger against the metal wiring. "Oh, Hampton," I said. "I'm so glad you came home. Where did you go?"

I studied Summer as she bit her lower lip so hard I thought it might bleed. She looked from Blake to me and back to him again.

"Summer took him!" Blake blurted.

"Blake!"

"She what?" I gasped.

"Summer took him for a walk."

"Summer?" I said, my voice firm. "Why would you do that?"

Summer's lip began to quiver. "I'm sorry, Birdie. Really, I am."

I sat down next to Summer on the bed. "Why would you do that? Blake was so scared."

"I know it was the wrong thing to do," she admitted. "But Hampton has been stuck inside this cage and in the cottage all summer. He's never been outside. He's never seen the ocean. I wanted him to see the ocean, Birdie. So he could feel free."

CHAPTER NINETEEN

JULY 29, 2023

RIVER FROST

It has been a week since I rescued Summer from Lawson at the Anderson cottage. I was starting to have feelings for her prior to that night, but if I'm being honest, those feelings multiplied by the hundreds after that brief amount of time we spent chilling in her motel room, and this scares me to death.

I was never the kind of guy to be nervous over dating, but considering I haven't dated anyone since Sarah, my stomach was doing nervous-ited flip-flops all morning because Summer and I have plans to go to dinner tonight. Neither of us have used the word "date," but then again, neither of us have said that this is not a date. I'm nervous for a few reasons, the biggest being that I owe it to Summer to tell her the truth. I need to tell her that I was married, and I need to tell her about Kinsley, which could very well be a deal-breaker for her. I also need to come clean about the night she called Blake. She needs to know that I'm the one who told her she should come home. By the time I am done with these conversations, there is a very big chance that she might not want anything to do with me at all.

But regardless of the outcome of tonight's dinner, I have really enjoyed this past week, just getting to know her. We haven't seen each other often, but every time I see her unexpectedly, she lights up like a Christmas tree, and her entire face glows. I recognize this in her because it is happening to me too. Our exchanges have been brief, but they have been fun, flirty, and filled with all sorts of tension that I have never experienced before. I like our banter, and I'm afraid that after tonight, what we have might change.

I retrieve my workbag from my closet and prepare to leave for the day, but I suddenly have an idea. I reach into the bag and pull out a black Sharpie marker, and I scribble something on the back of my service sign, the one that reads *Please Make Up Room.* I hang the sign on my doorknob after leaving the Sharpie on my dresser and head off to work, closing the door behind me, satisfied that now, even if tonight goes south, I have figured out a way to keep the momentum of our friendship moving in the right direction.

I BALANCE two trays of iced coffee under my chin while pushing the door to the warehouse open. Filming today is back in Portsmouth, and we have lots on the agenda. I am hopeful that we make good time so that I don't keep Summer waiting for dinner. My plan is to pump the entire staff with extra caffeine and keep everyone on track as best I can.

"Here you go," I say to Brad, handing him his iced coffee. I consider talking with him about the day off in August for Kinsley's play, but I know better than to ask him now.

He nods in thanks but doesn't look up from a script. He hands me a stack of call sheets and instructs me to hand them out. Just as I thought, we are starting the morning off with the filming of Sean and Cassidy and their hookup after

Sean's high school reunion. Considering Lawson and his costar had real-life practice hooking up, everything should go pretty smoothly.

I find Lawson sitting in a chair, reading over his script. I pass him his call sheet, and I try to avoid making eye contact with him, just as I have done for the past week. "Any of those coffees for me?" he asks.

"No."

"Okay, then," he says, raising his eyebrows. "So that's how it's going to be?"

"I don't know what you're talking about," I say with a shrug. "You didn't order one."

"Whatever."

"Just be ready in ten," I say, turning and walking away from him.

"Hey, PA!" he shouts, loud enough for heads to turn. "Next time you bring me a celebrity to bang, make sure she isn't a loser freak show."

The coffee tray crashes to the ground, and the sticky, icy liquid splashes on the cement floor. The blood begins pumping through my body rapidly, and I clench my jaw so tightly that I think I might break my teeth. I grab the collar of Lawson's white T-shirt with my left hand and draw my right fist back in preparation of punching him in the face, but instead, I take a step back, shake my head, and begin picking up what is left of the iced coffees. One of the cups remains half full, so I kick it in Lawson's direction. "Here's your coffee, asshole," I mutter under my breath, walking away. I hear clapping in the background, and I hope that the only thing that will keep me from losing my job will be the fact that I'm not the only one who wants to knock him out cold.

"Riv?"

I would recognize that thick Australian accent anywhere

—Brad. I turn to see Brad, the director, staring at me with his arms crossed over his chest.

Great, I think to myself. *I'm going to be fired on the spot.* I walk heavily toward Brad before dumping the empty coffee cups into the trash. "What's up, boss?" Maybe he didn't see me lose my cool. Maybe he wants to talk to me about something else. That could be the case, right?

Brad stares down at his clipboard, his expression serious. "Did I just watch you throw iced coffee on Lawson Remington?"

I tuck my hands into my pockets and shake my head. "No, man. I didn't *throw* coffee onto him. I sort of… kicked it at him."

Brad nods his head and remains expressionless as he looks up from the clipboard and meets my stare. "Did you punch him?"

"No. I definitely did not punch him."

He continues nodding his head and chews on the side of his pen. "Thena, my wife, told me what an arrogant prick he was to Summer Jennings."

"Yes, sir. He was a complete asshole."

"Thena also told me that you handled the situation discreetly. You were able to defuse the situation without anyone else catching wind about what happened?"

"That's correct."

"She mentioned that you and Summer have been spending quite a bit of time together."

"She's not wrong," I say through my involuntary goofy smile.

"Good. Thena and Oakley have both become very fond of Summer. Thena's birthday is next week, and I want to do something special for her. I have concert tickets at Fenway Park for August fourth to see Pink. We're taking a car in and staying over. Complete VIP meet and greet package. If we can find someone to watch Oakley, we're staying overnight in the city."

"Wow, that sounds—" Thoughts race through my mind at lightning speed. It doesn't sound like I'm getting fired, which is a huge relief. Summer is talking about me to Thena, which is even more exciting than not getting fired, and if Brad is making plans for August 4, that means we won't be shooting that day, which leaves a greater chance of me being able to watch Kinsley's play.

"We would love for the two of you to join us. It's nice that Thena has found a friend in Summer. And I'd also like to pick your brain over dinner. I'm working on a new project, and I'm impressed with your work."

I stand up straighter and raise my eyebrows. "Are you talking about—I mean, are you referring to my scripts?"

"Of course I've read your scripts, River. But I'm not just referring to that. I'm talking about your ability to control a chaotic and complicated situation. Lawson Remington is a walking chaotic and complicated situation, and you've handled him quite well, especially under the circumstances. If you're going to be an assistant director, you can't take crap from anyone, even your leading guy."

"Assistant director? Yeah, I hope to be that someday for sure."

"We will talk over dinner, then."

"Of course. August 4. I wouldn't miss it for anything," I say confidently, even though my insides are screaming, *Would you miss it for your daughter's summer-camp play?*

Brad begins to respond, but we are interrupted by a voice on the walkie. "We are rolling in five. Anyone have eyes on Lawson?"

I pause for a beat, allowing time for anyone to answer the call.

"Never mind. Found him making out with Robin from wardrobe."

"Thank you," I say into the walkie. "Rolling in five." I turn and begin to walk away from Brad, but he places an unexpected hand on my shoulder.

"Hey, Riv?"

"Yeah, boss?"

"Next time… punch him."

"Okay."

"You know I'm kidding, right?"

"Oh, okay," I say, running my fingers over my beard's scruff.

"But not kidding." He chuckles. "But your face was priceless." He laughs, jogging toward the set of Sean's bedroom, leaving me to process the whirlwind of information I have just taken in and wondering why all of a sudden, I find myself making promises that I can't keep.

CHAPTER TWENTY

I have two more rooms to clean before I meet Thena for lunch. I've been so consumed with my own thoughts this morning that I've made mistakes left and right. Not only have I managed to walk in on Mr. Thompkins getting dressed, which was not a pretty sight at all, but I've also forgotten to restock toilet paper and towels in most of the rooms. I'm hopeful that I can get through lunch without any guest complaints.

Although I'm both anxious and excited about my dinner with River, I am also still finding myself consumed with thoughts of Victor. It has been weeks since everything happened in LA, and he still hasn't reached out to me. Sure, he isn't my manager anymore, but I suppose I always considered him my friend. But silence speaks volumes, and Victor Diaz has been very silent. I wish the same could be said about my voicemail.

I've avoided dozens of calls from my agent, marketing coordinator, and publicist. I realize that I need to sort through the fallout from everything that happened in LA, but I just don't feel like I'm in a solid place to make any decisions right now. I miss Victor. Up until a few weeks ago, it would have been Victor I called to rescue me from messy situations like the one with Lawson. It was also Victor that I confided in over everything, both personal and professional. It's difficult enough being rejected by a person I considered to be the love of my life, but in the process of humiliating myself in that regard, I have also lost a friend. And losing a friend this close to me is something I have never really experienced, and I don't recommend it. How am I supposed to go from trusting him with my deepest and darkest secrets to not communicating with him at all? How am I supposed to just let this go and trust that he isn't going to blab everything I've ever told him in private? How long will it take to sort this out professionally? He was my manager for over six years. Surely this will be messy, which is probably why my agency wants to meet with me so badly.

I have one room left to clean, and it happens to be River's. I am pushing my cart up the porch ramp to his room when Blake stops me, balancing armfuls of toilet paper, wearing a scowl that would send a dozen hungry wild dogs scurrying away with their tails between their legs. "Summer."

"Blake."

"I've been running around all morning, answering calls from guests who are stranded on their toilets," he says, his expression humorless and his tone one of extreme irritation.

"Sounds like a personal problem," I say, cringing in disgust.

I begin to push past him toward River's room, but he places a stiff hand on my cart and stops me. "Did you restock any of the rooms today?"

"Did you forget to eat your Frosted Flakes today, Blakey? You seem a little cranky." I wrap my fingers around his wrist and remove his hand from my cart.

"If you're going to do this job, Summer, you need to do it right."

"Okay, Dad."

"Summer, I'm serious," he whines, his voice growing louder by the second.

I throw my arms over my head. "Then fire me, Blake, please! I didn't want this job in the first place. I just don't understand you!"

"You don't understand *me?* You show up here unannounced, and you expect to just live here like some princess. We need help, okay? So, sue me."

"Do you even remember talking to me on the phone the night of the party? Or were you so drunk that you don't even remember?"

He stares at me in confusion. "I—"

"You don't even remember," I accuse. "You were blabbing all about coming home and how it will be okay, and you gave me some stupid line about counting the stars."

Blake stands up straighter and narrows his eyebrows like he's trying to solve a difficult math problem. "Just, please do a good job," he says, tossing two rolls of toilet paper onto my cart. He storms away, stomping his feet in true little-brother fashion.

"Whatever, moron," I mumble under my breath. I turn my key in River's doorknob, laughing to myself that he remembered to put the sign on his door. I remove the sign and open the door. I hang the sign on the inside doorknob but pause when I realize that something has been scribbled on the back of it. It's a little smudged and hard to read, so I bring it closer to me, tracing my fingers over the chicken scratch. *One Call Away by Charlie Puth.*

I laugh out loud and hang the sign back on the door. I search the song on Spotify and secure my earbuds in place. I listen to the song as I make River's bed, fluffing the pillows as

I know he likes them fluffed. I clean his room in record time, smiling to myself as I listen to the song, some words tugging at my heartstrings and others filling me with joy. "Thank you," I whisper to the empty hotel-motel room. I play the song on repeat until I am finished with his room, and I prepare to head out to lunch, but I pause for a beat, having an idea of my own. I scan the room for the Sharpie, and sure enough, there it is on his dresser. I remove the marker's cap and grab the service sign. Right underneath his handwriting, I write the name of another song. I hang it back up on the doorknob and exit the motel room, thoughts of Victor beginning to dissipate as a feeling of excitement washes over me in anticipation of tonight.

* * *

"I CAN'T BELIEVE he still hasn't called… or even texted!" Thena exclaims. We are seated at a small table on the outside patio of the Sea-Pub, overlooking Long Sands Beach. Oakley sits between us in her high chair, chewing on the top of her sippy cup.

"I just don't understand how a person can go from being *your person* to simply being… nothing." I frown and take a bite of my salad.

Thena must notice the disappointment on my face because she seems eager to change the subject. "You must be so excited for tonight, though, right? Man, I'm, like, living vicariously through you."

This makes me smile. "Yes," I say, with confidence. "I am very excited for tonight."

"Where is he taking you for dinner?"

"I suggested York Harbor, but I'm not sure what he wants to do. Hopefully, they are done filming by then."

"You're speaking my language, sista," Thena says. "Story of my life."

I lift my arms over my head and yawn. "Maybe I should take a nap before tonight. Cleaning these rooms is kicking my butt."

"Just tell that little brother of yours that you quit."

"I totally should. I had a thing with him today. It's like he doesn't even remember talking to me on the phone the night of the party."

"Really? What makes you think that?"

"Well, because he can't remember anything he said to me. That night on the phone, he made it seem like coming home was the only thing to do. And then when I got here, he was shocked to see me."

"That's messed up. Had he been drinking?"

Oakley tosses her sippy cup to the ground. Thena bends down and grabs it.

"More!" Oakley squeals.

"I'm assuming so. Why else wouldn't he remember?"

Thena considers this for a moment. "He probably had too much to drink, and now he's embarrassed. I've gotten to know Blake. He's taking this management position very seriously."

"I know. It's just frustrating. If he had given me a little bit of tough love, like he usually does, I might not have left. I might have stayed and figured it out."

"And you would never have met me!" she says with a smile.

"Facts," I say, clinking my glass of sparkling water against hers.

Oakley throws her sippy cup into the center of the table and shouts, "Facts!"

Thena and I laugh together, but then her expression

grows serious. "I mean it, Summer. I was lonely before you showed up. I'm thankful I got to meet you."

"I'm thankful I got to meet you too. Thank you for being there. I'm not sure how I could have gotten through this without you."

"But seriously," she says. "On to more important topics. What are you wearing for your date tonight?"

"I haven't really thought about it."

"What? Girl, we need to get to the outlets, stat."

"I can't," I say, checking the time. I'm behind as it is, and I don't need another run-in with Blake. "I'll figure something out. Don't worry."

"Nope," she says, shaking her head. "This is a big night for you. If you won't let me take you shopping, then you will come raid my closet."

"I won't argue with that," I agree. And just like that, I've found a friend and a stylist in Thena.

CHAPTER TWENTY-ONE

JULY 29, 2023

RIVER FROST

The first thing I do when I get back to my motel room is check to see if Summer has moved the sign from the doorknob. Not only has she moved the sign, but she has also written back. Her handwriting puts mine to shame, and for a moment, I am embarrassed and hopeful that she could read my writing. She has written *Bryan Adams, Let's Make a Night to Remember,* and the title of the song alone is enough to make my heart feel like it is going to leap out of my chest. And it's also enough to send my stomach flip-flopping, setting off waves of nausea within me.

It is obvious to me that I am nervous about tonight because it is one of the first dates I have gone on since Sarah. And although I am really starting to like this girl, I am fearful that once the truth comes out, she isn't going to like me much, and this sends my thoughts flying in multiple directions. Why bother taking her out on a date if I am just going to be making confession after confession? Sure, the purpose of tonight is for her to get to know me and for me to get to know her, but she has already been through so much. I don't want to make things worse for her.

I'm in the shower, rinsing out the shampoo, when I hear my phone vibrating on the bathroom sink. I pull the shower curtain open and squint my eyes. It is a FaceTime call from Kinsley. I remember that I was supposed to call her after work this afternoon. I will call her back when I am finished showering. There is a piece of me that wants to share with Kinsley that I am taking her idol on a date, but another part of me, the part that knows better than to get a twelve-year-old girl's hopes up, decides against it. I'm also trying to avoid any conversation about attending her play on August 4, as I also committed to the business dinner with Brad.

I hop out of the shower, dry off, and wrap a towel around my waist. I am about to start shaving my face when I see a text come through from Summer.

> Summer: We still good for 7:00?

> River: You bet. I'm just getting out of the shower now.

A part of me considers what the outcome of the night might be if I don't confess to any of the secrets I've been keeping from her. How important is it for her to know that I have an ex-wife and a twelve-year-old daughter and that I pretended to be her brother when she needed him the most? Sure, the topics are important, but is it necessary that I bring them all up tonight? How much damage was done by my lying that night on the phone? I talked her off the ledge, literally, and I made her feel less alone. I do have to wonder, though. Would Blake have asked her to stay in LA and figure things out? Or would he have encouraged her to come home like I had? Does it even matter at this point?

I flip through the clothes in my closet and decide on a pair of dark-blue jean shorts and a burgundy button-down shirt. I check my reflection in the mirror and grab my phone to FaceTime Kinsley. There is a knock on my door, but after crossing my room and looking through the peephole, I realize it's Summer. She is standing outside my door, making eye contact with me as though she can tell I'm looking through from the other side.

"I figured I'd pick you up," she calls from outside. "It is 2023, after all."

I pull open the door, and I can't stop myself from smiling. She has this effect on me, Summer. "Hi," I say, my voice a bit shaky because she looks damn good, and I'm nervous as hell. She is wearing a short light-pink flowery sundress with a slit up the side. It's cut low in the front, and I feel the blood rush to my cheeks as I look her up and down and whistle. "Damn, girl. You look smokin'."

"Thanks," she says, gathering her hair over her shoulder. "You look smokin' too," she says, matching her tone to mine. "I hope you don't mind that I came over. I was just sitting in my room all alone, and I figured it was silly to just wait."

"It's more than okay. Let me grab my phone and my wallet, and we can head out."

"Perfect," she says, adjusting her purse over her shoulder.

We exit my motel room and head toward Brad's Maserati. We take off toward York Harbor for what I can only hope will be a fun and successful night, not the disaster that has played through my mind hundreds of times already.

CHAPTER TWENTY-TWO

JULY 29, 2023

SUMMER ROSE JENNINGS

We are finishing our appetizers at the York Harbor Inn when River and I finally start relaxing a bit. Our conversations have been brief, a bit awkward, and a little uncomfortable. At one point, when the two of us couldn't decide if we wanted to share a bottle of white or order our own drinks, the awkward silence was so overwhelming that I almost demanded we get out of there and go back to the way things were that night on my bed when I was snuggled in his hoodie and things just seemed simpler.

But I think we have found our groove. We have successfully ordered our entrees along with a second round of drinks and have been talking about my time in York as a child. I shared with him about Birdie and Papa and the strong influence they had on my life. I love that he had so many questions for me about growing up at the Anderson cottage and my time spent with Lark and Blake at the Seabird. I began to relax after my second glass of wine, and I think River did as well.

"So," he says, reaching across the table and taking my

hand in his.

This surprises me for a moment, only because I hadn't expected it.

He traces his fingers over the inside of my palm and holds his stare on mine. "I was wondering something."

"Okay?"

"I know we had huge plans to share our deepest, darkest secrets with each other. But if it's all the same to you, I was wondering—"

"I agree. Let's just keep it light." I breathe a sigh of relief, and I watch his shoulders relax. I'm happy because I really don't want to relive that night in LA on our first date, but I can't help but wonder what deep, dark secret River is hiding. I can't help it. I inhale deeply, let go of his hand, and say, "Just promise me you aren't married or seeing someone or anything that is going to come back and bite me in the butt," my words jumbling together in fragments.

River takes a swig of wine and smiles. "Okay, then. Looks like we're doing this." His tone is serious, but he is smiling at me, almost like he found my outburst amusing.

"So?" I ask.

He shakes his head and takes my hand back to his. "I don't have a girlfriend or a wife."

"Fiancée?"

"Nope."

I breathe a sigh of relief.

"But I do have an ex-wife."

For a moment, I think he is joking, but his expression remains still.

"I can't tell if you're joking."

"I kind of wish I were, but I'm not."

"Oh."

"Oh."

"Who is she?"

"Her name is Sarah. We met in film school out in LA. We were married right after graduation. Things got messy, and they didn't work out."

I nod, processing his confession. "You went to school in LA?"

"We both did. But when things changed for us, we moved to Boston."

"Together?"

"So, there's more."

"More?"

"I have a—"

River's confession is interrupted by the vibrating of his cell phone. It is a FaceTime call from someone named Kinsley. And Kinsley appears to be a cute little blonde with the widest blue eyes I've ever seen on a child, and it all comes crashing down on me like a million bricks all at once. "You have a daughter," I say so he doesn't have to.

"I should—"

"Take the call," I say, my tone calm and even-keeled. "It's totally okay."

"It is?"

"Sure, it is."

River swipes open the call, and he is greeted by Kinsley, who exclaims, "Dad! You didn't call me back."

"I know, baby. I'm sorry."

"It's okay."

I can't see her on the screen, but I am mesmerized by the light that has suddenly filled River's eyes. Every word he speaks to her comes out differently than the way I have seen him interact with anyone else. I find it hysterical that she is nailing him to the wall over not calling her back.

River asks Kinsley to hold on a moment, puts his phone to the side, and mutes the call. "I'm not going to tell her I'm out with you. If she knows that I've met you, let alone that

I'm out with you, she will lose her mind and will never go to sleep, and her mother will kill me."

"Oh, *she's* the superfan," I say with a smile, realizing that he knew every word and every chord to my song for his daughter's sake, and this makes my toes tingle and my heart flutter.

"Yes. And I really want her to meet you, just not like this."

"Understood."

River talks to Kinsley for a few more minutes before he tells her good night.

"I don't want to go to sleep, Daddy. I miss you," she whines.

River's face grows serious, and he nods his head. "I miss you too."

"When are you coming home?"

"I'm not sure. But remember, you're not alone."

"I just need to count the stars."

"Yes." He smiles. "Just count the stars."

My heart skips a beat after witnessing this exchange, partly because the way he speaks to her is the absolute sweetest, but also because I have heard this before. *If you are lonely, just count the stars... they will be the same stars I am counting... and you won't be alone.* River hangs up the call, and the waiter brings our dinners to the table. I ask for another glass of wine, sit up a bit straighter in my chair, and try like hell to pretend that I'm not in absolute shock from finding out about an ex-wife, a daughter, and a phone conversation I hadn't realized I'd shared with River Frost when I was at my worst.

* * *

ASIDE FROM RIVER'S shocking revelations, dinner was a success. I had shared with him my experience with Victor and what really went down that night at the party. He listened attentively, asking questions only when necessary and not judging me at all. If anything, he was angry for me. Frustrated because the story that was plastered all over the tabloids was a complete lie. He asked me if I was over Victor. I was surprised by his willingness to ask and the honesty that went into asking such a question, so I had simply shrugged and said, "I don't know. How do you get over someone when you don't even know if what you shared with them was real?" As far as I could tell, he had been satisfied with that response.

Although I still had a million questions about his ex-wife and his daughter, I had decided to save my questions about his history and parenting logistics for another day. One thing was for sure—Kinsley seemed sweet, and River appeared to be a great dad. Those two facts alone had canceled out any kind of negative feelings that might have come out of his revelation.

After dinner, we walked along Long Sands Beach. The tide had gone out just enough so that when we walked along the shore, the sand wasn't too hard or soft. It was simply just right, like the way I felt when he took my hand in his and we walked, simply enjoying the company of one another. Not asking any more questions, not contemplating life's biggest mysteries… just simply being together, alone, on Long Sands Beach.

Now, I sit on the edge of my bed, pulling my sundress over my knees, eager to get out of this outfit and back into River's stolen hoodie. I gather some more comfortable clothes from my dresser and find the hoodie folded up on the nightstand. I excuse myself, teasing that I am changing into something a little more comfortable and then make my grand entrance into the room. I'm dressed in black leggings and his gray hoodie. He finds this funny, and I like the way his face lights up when he laughs. He heads back to his room and returns in black athletic shorts and a new hoodie, carrying two Corona Lights.

"Perfect," I say, taking the beer from him, eager to snuggle up next to him like we had done the week before. "This is my kind of party."

"Oh yeah," he says, sipping his beer, hopping on my bed, and pulling my knees up into his hoodie. "I'm never going to get that back, am I?"

"Nope."

"Didn't think so."

I point at my guitar. "What are you going to play me tonight?"

"Oh no," he says with a smirk. "You're up."

I cringe and shake my head. "No, thank you."

"It doesn't work like that." He laughs. "I played you a song last time. This time, you play me one. I *am* a superfan."

"No. Your daughter is the superfan. You lose."

"Come on," he says, placing my guitar on my lap and sitting cross-legged next to me. "Play me something, anything."

"Fine," I say, tuning the guitar. "But I'm not playing any of my stuff. It just makes me too sad."

"Fair enough."

I finish tuning the guitar and retrieve a guitar pick in my nightstand. I begin strumming the strings, not sure yet what I'm playing for him, simply just strumming and watching him watch me. His whole demeanor shifts, and his expression softens, like somehow, just by playing this instrument, I have taken him to another place, which is something I've always loved about music. The joy of knowing I'm helping people escape from their realities, even if only for a few minutes, made all the hard work and sacrifice worth it.

My strums find a melody, and before I know it, I'm

playing "Somewhere in Between" by Lifehouse, the same song that was playing from my phone that night at the party. I close my eyes, and I feel each note. I relax my body as I start to sing, diving into each lyric that I have come to know so well over the years, feeling them in the deepest part of my soul. I allow the song to take over, to transform me into a completely different person than I was just moments ago. I'm not Summer Jennings anymore—I'm the song. I'm every note, every word, every beat.

When it is over, I'm afraid to open my eyes. But when I do, I am met face-to-face by a man whose eyes are glossy from tears and an expression that is foreign to me. Of course, I haven't known him long enough to know what all his faces mean, but I'm convinced that this one is an emotional concoction of admiration, awe, sadness, and even maybe, just maybe, love.

"Are you all right?" I ask, leaning the guitar against the wall and covering my head with the sweatshirt's hood.

He sits up straighter and motions for me to move closer. We are both sitting with our legs crisscrossed, our knees touching, his hands holding me under my elbows.

"I'm just fine," he says, his words catching in his throat. "That was beautiful, Summer."

"That's why they pay me the big bucks," I say with a laugh.

But River isn't laughing. "I mean it. I've never heard anything so amazing. You just *feel* it. Every note, every beat. It's truly incredible." His eyes are serious, like he's saying the most important thing in the world.

"Music… it's not just a thing to me. It's not just a hobby or a job. It's who I am."

He nods like he understands. Like I've given him the answers to all of life's greatest problems. "That's why, no matter what, you're always going to be okay, Summer

Jennings. Nobody can take that from you. Nobody can take away your music."

An unexpected and uninvited sob escapes from within me, and I quickly begin wiping my tears with the sleeves of River's sweatshirt. "Sorry," I say between tears.

"Don't be sorry. I'm sorry for getting you upset."

"I'm not upset. I'm just… I'm going through a lot right now. I'm worried the timing might just be a little off."

"I totally get it," he agrees. "But if there is one thing I've learned, it's that timing is never right." River takes my hand in his and pushes the sweatshirt sleeve up a few inches on my arm. He brings my hand to his lips and kisses my fingers. "I really like you, Summer. And I don't want all the noise and all our circumstances to get in the way of that."

My knees grow weak, and my heart begins to beat faster. Why does he have to say all the right things all the time? Part of me wishes he would just say the wrong thing so I can hate him like I hate Victor. Because I'm scared. I'm scared that I am going to open to Riv, and he is going to hurt me in the same way I was hurt by Victor. I'm not so sure I can survive another heartbreak, as I'm still nursing the first one. "I've been through a lot, Riv. And I can't guarantee that I'm even one hundred percent available. I mean, I'm not seeing anyone, but I was pretty into Victor. And I don't want to hurt you."

If Riv is upset by this, he doesn't show it.

"I get it. I know a thing or two about heartbreak. When someone you love lets you down to the extent that Victor has, it completely rocks your world and leaves you questioning everything. You just need time. Time heals all things, right?"

But the second he says this, I don't want time. I don't want to wait. I want him, and I want him *now*. But I can't move forward with him until I confront him about one last thing. "I… I know it was you."

"What was me?"

"That night on the phone. I know it was you and not Blake."

"Oh."

"Yeah, oh."

"Please don't be upset with me about that. Blake was completely wasted, and I—"

I place my finger over his lips and stop him midsentence. "It's okay."

"It is?"

"Yes."

"How did you know it was me?"

"'Cause I'm a secret spy for the FBI, and I hacked your phone." I wink. "Or I heard what you told Kinsley about counting the stars, and I remembered our entire conversation from that night."

He slaps the palm of his hand against his forehead and furrows his brow. "I'm an idiot."

"Well, that's how I knew." I lie down on my side, and he does the same.

"I'm sorry for lying to you."

"I wouldn't consider what you did lying."

"No?"

"No."

"You kind of… saved me." I inch closer to him and curl my knees into my chest. He wraps his arm around my waist and pulls us closer together. I take in the smell of him, and if I listen closely enough, I can hear the beating of his heart.

"I did?"

I nod my head. "When I left the party, I was devastated. Nobody was answering my calls, and I had never felt so alone. I'm not sure what I would have done if you hadn't helped me. And I'm pretty sure that knowing my brother, he wasn't going to take my call."

"He wasn't going to," Riv admits.

"I can't really put into words what it felt like to feel that alone. I trusted Victor, and I was left feeling like I imagined everything between us. I know he cared about me, but I think I cared more. I've come to the realization that even if he did have feelings for me, it didn't matter, because he loves Nova, and because of that, he threw me under the bus, and in hindsight, I don't really blame him. But in the moment, after drinking too much, I was at my worst."

"You were."

"So even though I wish you hadn't lied to me, Riv, I think it's kind of cool that you met me at my worst, and you still liked me enough to wait for me to find my way back… to my best."

River tucks a strand of hair behind my ear and smiles. I wait for him to say something, anything, but instead, he traces his fingers over my cheek, my jaw, and my lips. He places his hand behind my head and pulls me gently toward him until his lips meet mine, and we melt together in the perfect kiss. It isn't rushed. It's just the right amount of slow and the right amount of angst. It's like I've been running for miles in the peak of summer and I was thirsty and dehydrated and didn't realize I needed water. That is what this feeling is. Like River saw me dying of thirst and cracked open a fresh bottle of chilled Gatorade and was like, "Hey, here. This could help." His kiss is Gatorade. His kiss is everything. His tongue traces over mine then around my mouth, and we do this rhythmically, like we have mastered the perfect song after hours of rehearsal and have this finished product that we just can't wait to share with the world. Our kiss is magic.

River pulls back, and I don't have to wonder if he felt it

too. He looks like he wants to say something, but I need his mouth on me again, and I can't wait another second. I kiss *him* this time, and this time, it's deeper, heavier, faster. He pulls me on top of him, and I wrap my sweatshirt-covered arms around his neck, and he reaches underneath to hold my waist in his hand. His body screams at mine through his kiss, and there is no doubt in my entire being that he wants me as badly as I want him.

These feelings and these desires are new for me. I've never experienced a kiss like *that*, and although I want to experience a million more kisses with River like that, I feel like a tornado has ripped through me, tearing down the defensive wall I've worked so hard to build, and I need a second to catch my breath. I roll off him onto my back and cover my face with my hands. I stare up at the ceiling in awe. "Wow," I say, so overwhelmed by the power of a simple kiss that I can't find a better word than *wow*.

"*Wow* is right. Are you good?"

I roll onto my side and stare into his eyes. The truth is, I don't know what I want. I don't know what is too fast or what is too slow anymore. I've lost my grip on reality when it comes to love, loss, and everything in between. Part of me wants to curl up into a ball and go to sleep. It would be safer that way. We shared two kisses, the best two kisses I've ever had with anyone, so we could leave it at that and be fine, right? But what if being with him could be great? What if River is the one for me? What if I opened up to him and just surrendered? *What if?*

"What's going through that noggin of yours?"

I trace his nose with my pointer finger, and he smiles. "This is hard for me," I admit. "Letting you in."

"It's hard for me too."

"I want to trust you. I'm just so afraid of getting hurt. Getting your heart broken *sucks*."

"I'm scared too," he whispers. "But do you know what scares me more?"

"What?" I ask, my words sticking to the back of my throat.

"Not knowing *you*, Summer Jennings. The thought of never hearing you sing for me like that again, in that way, scares me. The thought of never kissing you again like that… scares me to death. Because that is how a kiss should feel." He fiddles with my sweatshirt's string and removes my hood from my head. He steadies my face with both of his hands in the gentlest, firmest way possible. I struggle to keep my eyes open and begin to surrender to his touch. I lean forward and place my hands on his shoulders to steady myself. "I'll sing for you again. Don't worry," I whisper in the darkness.

"And the kiss?"

"I will definitely kiss you again."

"So why aren't you?" His words come out deep, raspy, and bold. He's asking me a question, but he's also giving a direction. A command. He wants this, and he wants this now. He wants *me*.

I place my hands on the sides of his face and rub my fingers gently over the scruff on his chin and upper lip. I want more than anything to melt away into the darkness of the night with this man. But my heart still hurts, and my pain is so raw, and I promised myself I would never allow anyone to hurt me like Victor did. "River, I—"

I want to tell him that it isn't worth it. Taking a risk like this, putting yourself out there, and allowing another person to see you for who you really are, to know your emotions and your feelings, to let your guard down, to be vulnerable. It just isn't worth the risk. Because when push comes to shove, and you realize that you never really knew them, that the version of them you fell in love with is only an illusion, it is downright devastating and just not worth it.

"I have another confession," I whisper.

River narrows his eyes, and his jaw tightens. "You do?"

"River." I sigh. "This is going to come as a complete shock to you. But I love… your sweatshirt. And you're never getting it back."

River grabs me by the waist again and wraps my legs around his torso and is pulling me into him for the deepest, most passionate kiss of my entire life, and suddenly, I don't even know my name.

Riv's passion and desire, along with a yearning I have never felt before, echo through my entire body. His kiss, his touch, his movements feel so good, so right, that it becomes a longing and desperation within me that is almost too much. I want him so badly it hurts. His tongue fills my mouth until I can't take it anymore, but when he pulls away to kiss my cheeks, my forehead, and my chin, I pull him close again, desperately needing more. He teases me for a beat, softly grazing my lips with his, pulling back and doing so again until I find myself wrapping my hands around the back of his head and pushing his face against mine until I can feel him against my mouth again.

River removes the sweatshirt over my head, and I am left lying on my back in just leggings and a bra. He traces his fingers over my chest, and I gasp as he continues over my stomach, concentrating deeply, like he is taking in a work of art. He removes his own sweatshirt and is towering over me. I trace his abs and obliques, loving the soft moans that escape from him in response to my touch. He reaches his hands under my back and unclasps my bra, and I, too, am moaning as he tosses it on the floor.

River kisses me again, this time climbing on top of me. Our kisses grow faster and even more desperate. Our fingers and hands are moving in what feels like thousands of directions. I shimmy out of my leggings, and Riv removes his shorts. I roll over and pin him down on his back, surprising myself with my boldness. I hover over him, allowing the glow of the moon to highlight my face and my naked body. I pause for a beat, allowing him to take me in with his eyes, feeling sexier than I have ever felt in my entire life.

River reaches up and gathers my hair in one hand and grabs my lower back with his other. He whispers something to me about wanting me badly or needing me now, I can't really tell which, but he pauses for a moment. I watch him as he leans over the side of the bed and locates his wallet, and I silently thank him for being responsible because I've never cared less about birth control. But before I know it, he is kissing me again, and his lips are tracing over my neck, my chest, and my stomach. I pull him back on top of me and wrap my arms around his lower back. I resist the urge to close my eyes, and I lock my gaze on his as I pull him as close to me as humanly possible. My eyes remain locked on his until the sensations within me take over and I close my eyes, calling out to him in the stillness of the night, never wanting him to stop, never wanting him to let go. I dig my fingernails into his back, and he lets out a cry that sends me off into another dimension of happiness.

When it is over, he lies on top of me, burrowing his face into the crevice of my neck. I softly run my fingers through his hair and kiss him on the cheek. He responds by kissing my nose, my chin, and my neck. Our chests are still rising and falling to what feels like the beat of my favorite song. Our bodies are sweaty, and I tighten my grip on him, never wanting to let go.

"What's on your playlist, Summer Jennings?" he whispers in the deepest, sexiest way a man has ever spoken to me.

I think about this for a second and steady his face inches from mine. "*You are.* Right now, River Frost, you are the only song on my playlist." And with that, I roll him over and climb on top of him, kissing his neck and then his chest and move my mouth to his stomach, and he moans with pleasure. My lips trace back up his torso, and I'm eager for our lips to meet. And when they do, he slides his hands over my legs and up my thighs, stopping right where I want them to, and I cry out to him in a voice that I don't recognize, "River!"

This turns him on even more, and the sounds he makes in response to this puts me over the edge. He lays me on my side, moving his fingers over me, touching me in all the right places while he whispers all the right things into my ear, and I feel in this moment like I've completely left my own body. I'm studying us both from somewhere in another universe as he moves effortlessly over me in all the right ways, just as he did when his hands moved effortlessly up the neck of my guitar and his fingers had gently plucked the strings. I cry out again, trembling beneath him, pressing our foreheads together, and taking in the rise and fall of his chest against mine.

There are no words spoken in this moment. But I know without a doubt that we are making silent promises to each other. I study him through his intense stare, catch a glimpse into his soul, and decide in this moment that even though songs do make everything better and music is the greatest gift of all time, that people are the ones who make the music. And if given the chance, people can be surprisingly great too.

PART FIVE

AUGUST FOURTH

ONE WEEK LATER

CHAPTER TWENTY-THREE

AUGUST 4, 2004

MILLIE BIRD-JENNINGS

J was sitting on a bench overlooking the Nubble Lighthouse when Summer asked, "Birdie, do you ever get homesick?"

"Why?" I asked her. "Are you homesick? Do you miss your mom and dad?"

"A little bit," she admitted as she slurped the dripping ice cream from her cone. "I miss my mom, Dad, Lark, and my friends."

I nodded and studied the waves as they crashed along the shore. Being there at the Nubble Lighthouse with Summer always filled my heart with joy. It was times like this when she would open up to me about things that were bothering her or simply share her hopes and dreams. This was not something that came easy for her, so I always felt honored when she brought up things like this. "Yes," I admitted. "There are times I feel homesick."

"Like, when you are at the Anderson cottage, you miss your place at the Seabird?"

"Nothing like that," I admitted. "It's more like... if Grandpa Al goes away without me and I miss him. Or when you go home to Boston after spending the summer with me and I miss you."

"But those are people, Birdie. I'm talking about the kind of homesick you get when you miss your home."

"I understand," I said, passing her a napkin. "But I choose to believe that people feel like home."

I watched her as she processed this concept. She stared up at the Nubble, deep in thought.

"People can feel like home," she repeated as if she was locking it away in her memory. "You feel like home, Birdie."

"You feel like home, Summer Girl," I said, wrapping my arm around her lower back. "As long as we have each other, Summer, we will always be home."

CHAPTER TWENTY-FOUR

AUGUST 4, 2023

RIVER FROST

*S*ummer and I have spent every night together since our first date. That night will forever go down as one of the best nights of my life. I was certain that the second she found out about Sarah and Kinsley, she would be long gone. It was such a huge relief that not only did the idea of Kinsley fail to scare her away, I think it might have even made her like me more.

Summer had also been more than forgiving when she found out I'd pretended to be Blake on the phone. In hindsight, I think she is more embarrassed that she was so intoxicated that she couldn't tell the difference between Blake and me, which is a point I hadn't even considered until she mentioned it. The more I learn about the night in LA, the worse I feel for her. The more she tells me about Victor and what really happened, the more I want to punch him square in the face.

Now, we are curled up in my bed, wishing we could stay in each other's arms, under the blankets, and never get up. Summer is wearing another one of my sweatshirts and has informed me that she is keeping the other one, but since it has stopped smelling like me, I need to wear it again for a day or two and then give it back. I find her transparency and unapologetic demands regarding my favorite hoodies sweet —and a major turn-on.

We lie facing one another as I run my fingers through her thick brunette tresses. "I like your pink hair."

"It's maroon," she corrects. "But thank you. I kind of regret doing it."

"Why?"

Summer curls her ankles around my shins and nuzzles closer. "It was Victor's suggestion. I was getting ready for a photo shoot, the one promoting my 2024 tour, and he suggested a new look. The 2024 tour was going to be my biggest one yet."

This conversation is entering uncharted waters. We've avoided talking about her career, mostly because it makes her sad, and I hate to see her that way. There is also an underlying conversation that Summer and I have been avoiding. What does the future hold for us? When the filming of *The Hundredth Time Around* is over, I will most likely head home to Boston to be with Kinsley. Will she stay here? Will she go with me to Boston? Will she head back to LA, picking up where she left off? What will this mean for us? I have so many questions, but this isn't the time to ask. She is leaving for work soon, and we have our big night out tonight with Thena and Brad. So instead of asking her what will become of her tour, I simply nod and say, "Well, they are very pretty, the pink highlights. It was a good choice. No regrets."

"No regrets," she says with a smile, kissing me on the cheek.

"Are you excited about tonight?" I ask her.

"Absolutely. How are you feeling about everything?"

"Great, thanks to you." I wink.

"I didn't do anything. Thank Thena."

"But you talked to Thena, and if you hadn't, she wouldn't have brought it up to Brad, who wouldn't have suggested an early dinner. So, thank you."

"Anytime."

"You sure you don't mind that I'm missing the concert?"

"Of course I don't mind. You have your daughter's play. Will you Uber from there and meet us back at Fenway? Maybe try to catch the end?"

"Yes, ma'am," I say, pulling her in for another kiss, a longer one this time.

She showered here last night, and she smells like my favorite citrus agave shampoo.

I kiss the crevice of her neck, and she squirms beneath me, pulling away with a frustrated moan. "I have to go," she says, pulling back and wincing.

"No, you don't," I say, burrowing my face into her neck and pulling her close. "Tell Blake you can't work this morning."

"I've already told Blake I can't work this afternoon and this evening."

I reach my hands under her sweatshirt and lightly trace my fingernails along the small of her back. She moans again, this time covering her eyes with her palms and shaking her head from side to side.

"River," she whispers. "I have to go."

"What's ten more minutes?" I ask, sliding her hands off her face and wrapping her arms around me. My mouth meets hers, and I kiss her hungrily, deeply, because I might be too proud to beg with words, but my kiss is another story. She responds to this, kissing me back and reaching under my

T-shirt, digging her nails into my back, something she does often and that I can't get enough of.

"Fine," she says, her breath heavy. She pulls me back on top of her, wrapping her legs around my torso and running her fingers through my hair.

I lean in to kiss her again, but she puts her hand up as if to say stop.

"What is it? What's wrong?"

"Twenty minutes. And you're cleaning your own room today." And with that, she yanks my face down onto hers, kissing me with a longing and intense desire that is so powerful and passionate it catches me off guard.

"Deal," I say, pulling the sweatshirt over her head and tossing it away. "But by the time I'm done with you, Summer Jennings, you're going to be wishing you'd settled on thirty." I find the spot that I know she can't resist, and I watch as her back arches, her eyes close, and she gasps.

"Fine," she says between breaths. "I'll call in."

"That's what I thought."

"Let me text him," she says, reaching for her phone.

But I don't stop touching her. I don't stop kissing her. And she gives up on texting her brother.

"You're trouble," she says, her words catching in her throat.

"Trouble is my middle name," I whisper, chewing ever so slightly on her earlobe.

"No, it isn't," she gasps in response to my kisses, and it is driving me nuts.

"You're right. It's John. But you're mine for the day now, and I intend on taking full advantage of every..." My voice trails off, and I pull her on top of me in one quick sweep. I watch as she smiles and falls onto me, and it is in this moment, knowing that she is feeling the same way I do about us, that I am both relieved and filled with pure joy. Because I know deep in my heart that no matter what happens, no matter where we end up, that Summer is the one I am meant to be with. It is a certainty that I've never experienced before, and I am determined to make it work between us—some way, somehow—even if I need to beg, borrow, and steal to get us there.

CHAPTER TWENTY-FIVE

AUGUST 4, 2023

SUMMER ROSE JENNINGS

I have eighteen missed calls from my agent, ten missed calls from my marketing director, and fourteen missed calls from reporters, for a total of forty-two unanswered voicemails since I left LA. I've chosen to communicate very little with anyone over the last few weeks. Aside from talking with Tessa and Lark, I really haven't spoken to anyone outside of Thena, Blake, and River. *River.* If there could be a silver lining coming out of my experience in LA, it would be River. I have lost count of the number of things I love about that man. In the past, Tessa has accused me of looking for problems with the guys I've dated, and she wasn't wrong. But the only thing I could find wrong with River John Frost is that I can't seem to figure out how our future would work together. No matter how hard I try, I can't mentally picture a situation where I get to keep what is left of my career and River gets to keep shared custody of Kinsley, and that is a very difficult and uncomfortable place to be.

Blake tried to fire me this morning for not coming to work, but I bribed him with an autographed guitar pick that he could sell on eBay, and that seemed to do the trick. My geeky little brother even drafted a certificate of authenticity and had it notarized. But the hassle was worth it because the time I spent with River in his bed this morning was over-the-moon incredible. After half an hour had turned into an hour and a half, we finally got out of bed but went directly to his shower, where he proceeded to lather me up with the hotel bodywash until I was slippery and sudsy, and... well, that's a story for another day.

I put the finishing touches on my makeup and check the time. Brad's driver will be here at any moment, and we plan on getting to dinner early so Riv can make his escape to Kinsley's play. The plan is for Thena, Brad, and me to head into Fenway for the concert, and Riv will meet us afterward. He didn't invite me to watch his daughter's play, and in an effort to not make things awkward, I decided to just let things be. I realize that Kinsley wants to meet me, and I certainly want to meet her, too, but if there is anything I have learned about timing, it's that it needs to be right—or at least as close to that as possible.

My phone vibrates on my nightstand just as I am reaching for it. I have missed texts from earlier. I had checked in with Tessa this morning because it was a big day for her son, Bex.

Summer: How did Bex do today at the contest?

Tessa: He did so well! Thank you for checking! He placed second in his age group in short boarding, and he even scored a perfect ten on one ride. The perfect wave!

Summer: That's awesome! Desmond must be over the moon, excited.

Tessa: Oh yes. There will be celebrating for sure. What about you? What's on your playlist? 🎵🎵

Summer: I met someone.

Tessa: Who's that by?

Summer: No, LOL. It isn't a song. I met someone. 🖤

Tessa: OMG. Spill it.

Summer: I can't get too much into it right now 'cause I'm heading out. But he is amazing. I can't think of a song that captures what I'm feeling. Crazy, right?

Tessa: Who are you, and what did you do with my friend? 😲

Summer: Catch up tomorrow?

Tessa: Of course.

Summer: Tell Bex I said congrats!

I SLIP my phone into my purse and check my outfit in the mirror one last time. I've decided on a maroon strapless top with my favorite ripped cutoffs. I nod at my reflection in approval but decide last minute to grab a long-sleeved shirt from my closet. I'm reaching into my closet when there is a knock at my door. It's not a River knock, and it isn't house-keeping because, well, I'm housekeeping.

"Hold on a sec," I call from my closet. I panic for a moment, thinking that maybe everyone is outside waiting for me, or Brad's driver has come to retrieve me. I grab keys and my purse and swing open the door—and I stop breathing.

"Hey, Sums."

Victor. Victor Diaz is in the doorway of my motel room. Victor Diaz has his hands in the pockets of his white shorts and is staring at me beneath the rim of his LA Rams cap, his eyes flickering with specks of something unfamiliar. Guilt? Shame? Regret? I try to find words, any words, but I come up short, so instead, I just shake my head and form the name *Victor* with my mouth and slap my palm to my forehead in disbelief.

"Can I come in?"

The room begins to spin, and I brace the door's frame for support. My knees grow weak, and I want to crumble to the floor. But then I look up at him and see his face. This is the same person that guided me through the Hollywood chaos for years. These are the same eyes that smiled at me across the dinner table with his family at Sunday dinner. These are the same lips I kissed just weeks prior. He is the same Victor I have always known. But he is also the same Victor who has ghosted me since the most humiliating night of my life. He is the same Victor who threw me under the bus to the media, to my fans, to everyone. "I'm sorry, no," I say firmly. "I have plans. You need to go."

"I just flew across the country."

"Well, you should have called," I say with a shrug. "I would have been happy with a text message, or even a thumbs-up emoji. Wait. Is there an I'm-sorry-for-being-an-asshole emoji?"

I squeeze between him and the door, eager for this awkward encounter to come to an end. The last thing I need is for River to approach him. Knowing what he knows about Victor, I can't imagine it would play out well for anyone. Victor places a sturdy hand on my shoulder. I turn and meet his stare. "What?"

"Where are you going?"

CHAPTER TWENTY-FIVE

"I'm going to a concert."

"You're going to a concert."

"Yes. Do you have a problem with that?" I'm completely aware that I sound like an obnoxious teenager throwing shade at an angry parent, but I'm losing my ability to see this situation clearly. His betrayal is still a fresh, open wound, and his presence has added salt to it—and it stings like hell.

"Yes, Summer. I do have a problem with you going to a concert."

"Why?"

"Because you *are* the concert. You have a tour to plan."

I stare at him, wide-eyed. "How did you even know where to find me?" I ask, taking a step outside onto the porch.

"It wasn't that hard. There were only so many places you could be. Plus, I reached out to your brother, and he told me where to find you."

"That moron," I mutter under my breath.

"He's not a moron. He's worried about you."

"Well, he has a funny way of showing it."

Victor takes a step outside and clasps my hand in his. "*I'm* worried about you, Summer."

"I'm sorry. What?"

"The agency called. They are canceling your tour if they don't hear from you within the next twenty-four hours."

I release his hand from mine and stare at the ground, crossing my arms over my chest. "Okay," I say.

"Okay?"

"I'm fine with that. I have to be."

I turn and walk away from him, leaving him standing outside my room. "Please close the door," I say with more sass than I intend. "Have a safe flight home."

I hear my door close, followed by footsteps behind me. I spot Brad's driver standing outside a black SUV. Brad is in the passenger seat, Thena is in the second row, and River is nowhere to be found. "Summer, please," Victor begs. "Talk to me?"

"On what planet would I want to talk to you?"

Thena exits the car and appears by my side. She wraps her arm through mine and holds my hand. This gesture is so kind and affirms how much I care about her friendship, and because of that, I can't hold back the sob that has been stifled deep within my chest for the past twenty minutes.

"I'm thinking you should leave," Thena says calmly but with authority.

"I think that's probably best for everyone," a voice behind me agrees—River.

Victor studies Riv and gives him a solid once-over. "I'm not leaving until you talk to me, Summer."

"It's not a good time," I say, my voice quivering with each word.

"When would be a good time, then? When the tour gets canceled? When all your hard work goes to crap?"

"They are canceling your tour?" Riv asks, his eyes filled with concern.

I stare at the ground and lean my head on Thena's shoulder. "Yup."

"Not officially," Victor explains. "Summer hasn't returned any of the phone calls. They reached out to me because they thought I might be able to help."

"What does she need to do?" Riv asks, his voice steady.

"She needs to call them back, man."

River nods. "By when?"

"She has twenty-four hours."

I clench my fists to my sides. I'm not okay with this. I don't like that they are talking about me like I'm not here. I don't need River asking these questions on my behalf, and seeing Riv and Victor together just confuses me in so many ways. I look from Riv to Victor and back to Riv. "I'll call them when I'm ready," I say. I look at Thena, and we both get into the SUV. "We have a dinner to get to," I say. "Talk to Blake if you need a place to stay."

"When will you be back?" Victor asks.

"Tomorrow around noon."

"Can we talk then, please?"

River gets into the car, and Victor approaches my window. He taps on it and motions for me to roll it down. I don't, but the driver does. "Tomorrow? I'll come back, and we can talk. Please?"

"Okay," I say, losing the ability to stand my ground.

"Around noon?"

"Around noon."

"Summer?"

"What, Victor? What do you possibly have to say for yourself?"

"I'm sorry."

CHAPTER TWENTY-SIX

AUGUST 4, 2023

RIVER FROST

We are seated at a table overlooking Hanover Street in the north end of Boston, at my favorite Italian restaurant, Dolce Vita. Thena and Brad are seated across the table from Summer and me. We have already devoured our appetizers, consisting of homemade bruschetta, fried calamari, and stuffed mushrooms. The owner is bringing out our second bottle of red wine and is refilling our glasses when Summer reaches under the table and takes my hand. I nod at her and, with my eyes, ask her if she's okay. She smiles at me in return, and I get the sense that she is holding on by a thread.

I'm proud of her for the way she handled Victor earlier. I saw him approach her door and decided it would be best to let her handle it, and she did. She is stronger than she real-izes, for sure. The dude had some nerve showing up out of the blue like that. He could have called or texted her, and in my mind, the only reason he wouldn't have the guts to do that would be because he knows he was wrong.

I would be lying if I said I wasn't nervous about tomor-row. The idea of the two of them hashing things out has left me uneasy, to say the least. It's been over ten years since I've felt this way for anyone. Sure, there was a time when I was head over heels for Sarah, but once that ended, especially in the way that ended, I never thought love would be in the cards for me again. But here I am, sitting hand in hand with the most beautiful woman I have ever laid eyes on. And we've shared the most amazing week of my life together. But Victor and Summer have a history, a history that well surpasses one week at a motel in Maine. I would be naïve to think she could forget about the feelings for Victor that have stirred within her for years. Hell, she even warned me on our first night together that she didn't know if she was over him. I wouldn't be upset with her if she gave him a chance. I would be devastated, to say the least, but I wouldn't blame her one bit. As much as I don't like the guy, he did fly across the country in support of her career. Summer has worked too hard to give up the one thing she loves—music. Knowing that she might lose her career over the rumors that stemmed from that party fires me up in more ways than I can explain.

"So, River," Brad starts. "Mind if I interrupt this great time to talk a little shop?"

Summer rubs her hand on my knee as if to say, *You've got this*. "Yeah, man, of course." I take a sip of my wine and raise my glass. "I'm all ears."

"Like I mentioned before, I'm working on a new project. It's a TV series, which is out of my wheelhouse, but I've met with the writers, and it sounds really promising."

"Awesome," I say. "Mind if I ask what it's about?"

"It's a police crime drama," he says. "About a cop who changes careers and becomes a private investigator. And it takes place here in Boston."

My mouth drops open, and I feel my eyebrows rise. "That's really great," I say. "And you've read the script?"

"I have," he says, nodding. "I'll email you the info for the first season. Look at the sizzle reel and let me know what you think. I've got some big names lined up for this one. If you're interested in being my AD, I could use some boots on the ground out this way while Thena and I sort things out back in LA. Thena mentioned you are interested in staying here, in the city, with your daughter. I think it could be a steady, long-term fit for you."

"Thank you so much," I say, unable to contain the smile that has grown across my face.

"Take some time to think about it," he says, glancing from me to Summer. I side glance at Summer, who looks genuinely thrilled for me, but I can't help but wonder what's going through that mind of hers.

"Of course. When do you need to know by?"

"Take the week. I need to let the network know what I've decided by then."

"Copy that," I say in my best cop-sounding voice.

"Copy that," Brad says with a smile.

The four of us raise our glasses and cheer new friendships, new opportunities, and endless possibilities.

* * *

WE ARE PAYING the tab when Summer excuses herself to use the restroom. She leaves her purse at the table but takes her phone with her, and I can't help but wonder who she might be texting or calling. I know it's none of my business, but between Victor's surprise visit today and the job offer I just received in Boston, I feel like Summer is slipping through my fingers, and I am desperate to stop it.

When ten minutes pass and she doesn't return, I decide to check on her. "Excuse me," I say, rising to my feet. "I need to use the restroom too."

Thena gives me a thumbs-up and a wink, like she is

silently rooting for me. I jog down the stairs and through a narrow hallway where Summer is exiting the restroom and sees me heading toward her. She tries to smile, but it is clear to me that she has been holding back tears.

"Riv—" she starts, shaking her head and wiping the tears from her eyes. "I really just needed a minute."

"Then take it," I say, pulling her back inside the bathroom and locking the door behind us. "Take a minute."

She sobs into my chest, apologizes for getting tears on my white button-down, and cries some more. "I'm so sorry," she sobs. "This is your big night, and I'm making it about me."

"It's not just my big night," I whisper. "It's our big night."

She looks up at me for clarification. "It is?"

I bury my face on the top of her head and hold her tighter. "I'm just going to say this," I say, inhaling her sweet scent. "I've never met anyone like you, Summer. And I really don't want to lose you."

"You don't?"

"No, I don't. I'm not making any decisions about this job until *we* talk about it together."

"But there is so much…"

Her voice trails off, and someone knocks on the bathroom door. "Just a minute!" I holler. I pull the hair back from her face and kiss her forehead. "Summer, I know you have a history with Victor. I realize today must have been brutal for you. And I appreciate it so much that you still came here with me… for me. We are going to get through this together, okay?"

"Okay," she agrees between sniffles.

"Are you okay?"

"I will be."

"What's on your playlist?"

She breathes a sigh of relief, like she's thankful I know

how to speak Summer. "Third Eye Blind. 'How's It Going to Be.'"

"Yikes," I say, laughing nervously. "That doesn't bode well for me."

This makes her smile, and she stands on her tiptoes, reaching up for a kiss. There is a knock on the door again, louder this time, so I pull away from her and wipe her eyes with my thumbs and pointer fingers. "So I know you are really into Pink and all, but there is a twelve-year-old little blond girl that is about to knock it out of the park as Elle Woods, and if you would join me at her performance, it would mean the world to both of us."

The smile on Summer's face exceeds anything I could have expected. She jumps up and throws her arms around my neck and squeals. "Really? You mean it?"

"Of course I mean it."

"River Frost, I thought you would never ask."

CHAPTER TWENTY-SEVEN

AUGUST 4, 2023

SUMMER ROSE JENNINGS

We are standing outside the theater, holding pink roses that Riv purchased at the venue. We sat in the back of the theater for Kinsley's performance, and it is dark outside, so thankfully, nobody has recognized me. Kinsley Connors-Frost completely stole the show, and I can't wait to tell her how beautiful and talented I think she is.

"Your daughter is amazing," I whisper to Riv, who is wrapping his hand around mine.

"She is, isn't she?" he agrees.

"Thank you for bringing me," I say. "I know you are taking a leap of faith here."

"You make leaping easy," he says with a wink. "I probably should warn you. You are about to meet my ex-wife," he says through gritted teeth and a fake smile.

"Huh?" I ask, standing up a bit straighter and wrapping my sweater around my strapless top. "She's here now?"

"Uh-huh," he says, gesturing toward a tall blond woman heading in our direction. She's naturally pretty in an "I don't need to wear makeup to be pretty" sort of way.

"River," she says with a polite nod and a hug meant for distant family on forced holiday get-togethers. "You made it."

"I promised," he said with a shrug.

"And you brought a guest," she says, looking in my direction. I extend my hand to hers for a handshake. She takes my hand and pauses for a beat, and I realize that I've been made.

"Are you—"

"This is Summer," Riv says, completely downplaying the fact that he has brought his daughter's favorite Hollywood celebrity to her summer-camp play.

"I… I know," Sarah says, standing up a little straighter. "Summer Jennings. It's nice to meet you," she says, gaping up at River in disbelief.

"Is Tom here?" River asks, referring to the man I assume is Sarah's husband.

"He's home with Luke," she says, frowning in disappointment. "Luke came home from camp with a fever. They couldn't make it."

"Sorry to hear that," I say. "Your daughter is so talented. You should be proud."

"Thank you," she says. "I'm sure she will appreciate you being here. How do you two…" Her voice trails off because Kinsley is rounding the corner, and she is sprinting toward River at lightning speed.

"Daddy!" she cries. "You made it!"

River passes the flowers to Sarah just in time for Kinsley to leap up into his arms. He picks her up and spins her around, happiness glowing from them both, shining like the brightest stars on the darkest night. "I told you I would." He chuckles. "You were amazing," he says, kissing her on the cheek. He sturdies her feet back on the sidewalk and points at me. "I brought you someone," he says, his expression nonchalant and overly calm.

Kinsley turns to me and smiles, and when she processes

everything, she freezes. Her mouth gapes open, and her eyebrows rise up, and I recognize this expression because it is the same way River looks when he is surprised.

Kinsley squeals and jumps up and down. "You're… Holy crap, Dad. This is… Summer Jennings?" She throws her arms around my waist like she has known me forever. She pulls back, squeals again, and hugs me. This goes on for over a minute before Sarah saves me. She gently pulls Kinsley back and whispers something in her ear. Kinsley looks up at me and gasps. "You saw my play?" she asks.

"Yes, I did," I say. "You are a star for sure."

"Thank you, Summer," she says in disbelief. "Dad, where did you find her?"

He thinks about this for a beat, and I side glance at Sarah, who is also very curious about his answer.

"You're never going to believe it if I tell you," he says, placing his hands in his pockets and staring up at the sky.

"Tell me," she begs. "Please. And then we need to take a selfie."

I chuckle at this and study River's expression. Parenting looks good on him. He loves Kinsley more than life itself, and there is no denying this. "She called me one night," he begins, choosing his words carefully.

"She did?" Kinsley asks, intrigued.

"She did," he says.

They both look at me for confirmation. "Yes, I did."

"Why did you call my dad?"

"I—"

"Because she was lonely," he says for me.

"Oh," Kinsley says, considering this for a moment. "You're a good one to call when you're feeling lonely. Did you help?"

"Yes, I did," he says, reaching for my hand and touching it to his lips. "I was sad and lonely because I was missing you. Summer called me right at the exact moment I was counting the stars. We counted the stars together, and then we were both happy again. Wouldn't you know it? A few days later, she was standing at my doorstep."

If my heart were any fuller, it would burst out of my chest.

Kinsley wraps her arms around me once more and cries, "Thank you, Summer. Thank you for helping my dad."

I smile the biggest smile and stare up at Riv, who couldn't look any happier if he tried. I snap a selfie with Kinsley and autograph her program for the play and insist that she autograph mine.

Sarah takes a photograph of River, Kinsley, and me and promises to find me on social media. "Thank you," she whispers to me as she hugs me goodbye.

At first, I think she is thanking me for surprising Kinsley, but when I catch the glimmer of happiness in her eyes as she studies River and his beaming smile, I know in my heart she is thanking me for more. Much, much more.

PART SIX

AUGUST FIFTH

ONE DAY LATER

CHAPTER TWENTY- EIGHT

AUGUST 5, 2023

MILLIE BIRD-JENNINGS

$\mathcal{A}$l and I were crossing the border from Arizona to New Mexico in our RV when Summer called yesterday evening. Considering Al and I are not huge fans of technology, we have only the one simple black prepaid phone that Violet insisted we purchase for our road trip across the country. It was for use in case of emergency, and lucky for us, we had yet to experience an emergency, so imagine my surprise when it began to ring from the dashboard of our RV.

"Hello?" Al had answered. "Summer? Summer, how are you? We are over in your neck of the woods, you know." He was silent for a moment and covered the phone with his hand.

"Watch the road!" I had scolded.

If he heard me, he pretended not to. "It's Summer. She sounds upset. She wants you."

"I took the phone from him and placed it to my ear. "Summer? Hey, girl!"

"Hi, Birdie," she said between sniffles.

"What's wrong, dear? Are you all right?"

"I only have a minute," she had told me. "I'm… I'm actually in the bathroom of a restaurant in Boston."

"Boston? What are you doing out east? We thought you were still out in Hollywood. I was going to call you when we reached Cali."

"I know. I'm sorry I didn't tell you. There is a lot you don't know, Birdie. I'm back home working… working for Blake at the Seabird."

"Well, it sounds like we need to catch up, then," I had said. "When you have more time, that is."

"Yes," she had agreed. "But Birdie, I just really needed to hear your voice."

I side glanced at Al, who could see the concern written all over my face. "What's going on?"

Summer filled me in regarding the events of the past few weeks. She briefly told me about her manager, Victor, and the feelings she had developed for him over the years. She told me about the events that took place at the reunion party and of the decision she needed to make regarding her career. It was only when she mentioned the new man she was seeing, River, that she became so emotional that she was unable to explain her situation in words.

"Do you love either of them?" I had asked, because when Summer lost her ability to find her words, it was best to be direct.

"Yes. I think I love them both."

"I see."

"Birdie," she asked, muffling back a sob, "how did you know that Grandpa Al was the one? You were always so certain it wasn't Philip."

"Oh, Summer." I sighed. "This isn't the first time you've asked me this question."

"I know, Birdie."

"I think it's time you search within yourself for this answer. I can only tell you that from the moment your grandfather kissed me under the night of the Nubble Lighthouse, I knew he was the one for me. It wasn't so much the words he spoke, but it was more in his touch, his kiss. I knew because when I looked into his eyes, they were the eyes of a man who loved me for me."

"And you have no regrets?"

"No regrets."

"I just don't know what I'm supposed to do now. I'm talking with Victor tomorrow, and I know he is going to ask me to go back to LA. My music career, Birdie. It's everything I ever wanted."

"And the other boy. River?"

She was silent for a moment before she said, "I really want you to meet him. He loves York, he loves your motel, and he really loves your cookies."

"Well, then, he sounds like a keeper for sure. Listen to your heart, Summer, and you will find a way. You've always been a smart girl. But you need to start listening to your heart and trusting yourself. Your love for music is what got you through tough times in your past, but maybe it's time to stop hiding behind it and listen to what you know is right for you."

"Thank you. It's just all so hard. I'm so scared of being hurt."

"You are stronger than you think, Summer. Don't ever forget that."

"Like the dancing grass," she had whispered.

I closed my eyes and remembered the day outside the arcade, when we watched the grass dancing in the breeze. "That's right. You are strong. And you are enough. Never let anyone take that away from you."

Summer had thanked me and promised to keep me posted. I told her I loved her and to call me anytime. I had informed her that I wanted to send her a postcard from one of the states we had visited. When I asked her if I should mail it to LA or Maine, she hesitated. "Can you just send two? One to Maine and one to California? That way, I will be sure to get it."

* * *

Now, Al and I are just finishing breakfast at a diner we discovered in New Mexico. Al is biting into his last piece of bacon when he asks, "Have you heard from Summer again?"

I take a sip of my coffee and shake my head. "No, Al. I haven't."

"I'm worried about her."

"Don't be. She is strong."

"I picked this up," he says, pulling a magazine out of a Target shopping bag. "Our granddaughter is on the cover."

I study the cover and shudder as I trace my finger over Summer's side profile. "This is Victor," I say.

"He looks like a complete moron!" Al barks.

"Well," I start. "If Summer sees something in him, then I trust he is a good person."

"Have you spoken with Violet about this? Or Lark?"

"No, but they are all down in Florida. They aren't in New England with Summer."

"What about Blake?"

I consider this for a moment. If Summer is working for the motel, then Blake would be the one to know the most about what is going on, right? "I'll call him when we get back to the RV. Would that make you feel better?"

"Yes, it would," he says with a nod.

"She's going to be okay, you know," I say, taking his hand

in mine and smiling. "Our girl is a fighter. Once she discovers her own strength within herself, she will be unstoppable."

CHAPTER TWENTY-NINE

AUGUST 5, 2023

SUMMER ROSE JENNINGS

*I*f I could have stayed in that moment with River and Kinsley forever, I would have in a heartbeat. But all good things come to an end. I mean, they can be followed by making it to Fenway Park in time for Pink's celebrity meet and greet, followed by a night in the penthouse of one of Boston's swankiest hotels, but they still come to an end, and that can be a huge letdown. It can also be an even bigger letdown when it is followed by a meeting with your ex-manager- slash-fake-best-friend the next day.

As much as I wanted to meet with Victor in public, we both decided it would be best if we kept a low profile. So now, we sit on the sofa in my room, sipping motel coffee. Leaving River prior to our meeting was extremely emotional and somewhat heartbreaking. We had kissed goodbye in his room, and he rambled on and on about me needing to do what's best for my career and not to hold back because of him. He had kissed me on the forehead prior to his departure and whispered, "You are stronger than you think." This meant more to me than he ever could have imagined. I had thanked him by kissing him as long and as hard as I could, searching within the deepest corners of my soul for evidence that the kiss did not mean goodbye.

"I'm listening," I say to Victor, sipping my coffee and meeting his gaze.

"I want to start by saying I'm sorry. I'm sorry for any confusion I may have caused you over the years."

When I'm silent and he realizes I'm going to remain that way, he continues.

"Nova and I, we had our differences. But I always had every intention of being faithful to her."

I nod and grimace. "I know that, Victor. And I never disrespected Nova."

"I know," he says, growing frustrated with me. "Can you let me get this out?"

"Go ahead."

"You and me, we have something special. I know that. We just click, you know?"

I nod in agreement, as painful as that is to admit at this point. "Yeah," I say. "I know."

"But Nova, she's the love of my life. And when she broke it off with me, it crushed me. And you were there for me, and when I was with you, Summer, it just… it hurt less."

"I can see that," I say, thinking about River and how the pain I was feeling when I first came home was so incredibly agonizing until I met him.

"I know I should have been more professional with you. And I know I led you to believe that we could be more. And if I'm being honest, there were times that I did want more. I'm sorry that I gave you the wrong idea. And I'm even sorrier that I handled things the way I did that night at the party."

I study him, intently, and suddenly, all the feelings and emotions that have followed that night in LA burst out of me at the seams. *Liar,* I think to myself. Suddenly, my entire history with Victor flashes before my eyes. Our intimate conversations, the flirting, the touching, the simple desire and satisfaction in just simply being together. I slam my coffee mug down on the table and cross my arms over my chest. "I'm not buying it, Victor. You have a lot of nerve showing up here after all these weeks with some bullshit line about me being your shoulder to cry on and nothing more. At least man up and tell me the truth."

"Summer—"

"Screw you, Victor. We had a connection, you and me. You *wanted* to be with me. You were just too chickenshit to face your feelings, and shame on me for letting you do it. I know what I was experiencing with you was real, so just do me a favor and be honest with me. You were in love with me. You *are* in love with me. I was never alone in this, and you know it." I'm pointing my finger in his face when a tear escapes from his eye. "You were in love with me," I repeat again.

"Okay," he says, reaching for his water glass. "Okay, you're right. I *do* care about you."

"You love me."

"Okay, fine, Summer. I love you."

"And you have for a while. I did not make it up. You led me on, you messed with my emotions, and when Nova left you and things got too real, you hid behind me."

Victor is silent for what feels like hours. He takes another sip of water and rubs his hand through his hair. "Okay," he says, his voice sounding defeated and frustrated. "You're right. And I'm sorry. How can I make it up to you?"

"Make it up to me?" I laugh like he has told the funniest joke in the world. "It's done, Victor. You made a fool out of me. The world thinks that I broke you and Nova up. The world believes the lies you told."

"What if I come clean?"

"Come clean"

"If I come clean—we talk to the reporters, we both agree to comment, clear the air—will you go back to LA? And do your tour?"

"How could you come clean? What would that do to Nova?"

He stares down at the ground and shakes his head. "We broke it off. For good."

I don't know why this changes things for me. This shouldn't change things for me. But hearing that Victor broke it off with Nova sends me downward spiraling in a million different directions. If Victor is single and he flew across the country to talk to me, this means that there is a chance he is here not only for professional reasons but also for obvious personal reasons too. I rub my eyes with the backs of my hands. "Victor, I'm exhausted. Can you please just tell me like it is? Why are you here? What do you want? I can't see this situation clearly until I know what I'm working with. You owe me that much."

He inches closer to me on the sofa and takes my hands in his. He clears his throat and starts to speak but stops. He closes his eyes like he is counting to ten before inhaling, exhaling, and opening them back up again. "I came here for you, Summer. I want to be with *you*. It's always been you. And I... I want the life we were sharing together, but more. I want to know what it is like to be with you in all the ways we haven't experienced together. When you kissed me that night at the party, I felt it too. You're right. You're not in this alone. When you kissed me that night, it rocked my world, but it also scared me to death."

I'm crying before I let his words sink in. "Your timing sucks," I say, shaking my head in disbelief. I stand up, make my way over to my bed, find River's sweatshirt, and pull it over my head. I sit back down on the couch and wipe the tears away with the sweatshirt's sleeve. "I met someone."

"I know."

"He's amazing."

"I know."

We are both crying now, and seeing him like this just breaks me. I revert to my old Victor Diaz ways and crumble, wrapping my arms around his shoulders and crying into his neck. Just like I did the first time I read a negative review of a performance and all the other times he was there for me—as a manager, a friend, and more. Sure, this guy was a complete jerk and all but ruined my career and dropped me the second things got hard, but we have a history together. And even though he did all those crummy things to me, doesn't it count that he's done a ton of really great things for me too?

"I'm so sorry, Summer. I'm so sorry."

We weep together there in my motel room, where I find myself back at square one, crying over Victor Diaz and what could have been, only this time, it is in the arms of Victor Diaz. This continues until I excuse myself to go to the restroom so I can wash my face and take a minute to process it all, because the ball appears to be in my court, and it looks like I have some choices to make. I could head back to LA with Victor, pick up where we left off, clear our names with the press, and have my tour. Isn't that everything I ever wanted? It was, yes, but then I met River.

I could stay here on the East Coast with Riv, and even though we've only just met, River feels like the only person who has ever really seen me for *me* without even trying. And I adore Kinsley. I can picture myself being a part of her life in so many ways. The idea of sharing someone like Kinsley with a man like Riv makes my heart burst with joy. But how well do I even know River? Aren't I getting ahead of myself here? And where would that leave my career? Could River be my rebound? What if that's all he is and I throw away an entire career and relationship with Victor, whom I very recently believed to be the love of my life?

I swing the bathroom door open and pace around my room. "So, what exactly am I supposed to do here?"

"Um, come home?"

"It isn't that easy."

"Blake says you've been cleaning motel rooms, Summer. It kind of is that easy."

"Blake's a moron!" I snap. "I've built a life here. Sure, I don't have a rooftop pool or a concert tour, but I've found something special here."

"You found something special at the Seabird Motel?"

"Maybe. What's wrong with that?" I challenge.

"Because the Summer Jennings I know is a Hollywood celeb. The Summer Jennings I know drinks sparkling water poolside while she writes hit songs for a living. The Summer I know wouldn't be caught dead staying at the Seabird Motel, let alone cleaning its toilets."

"Wow, Victor… just, wow."

"I'm not trying to take anything away from you. You came home to a place that has always been special to you, and that's great. But don't forget who you are, Summer." His words hit me harder than he probably meant them to.

"Maybe that's the problem," I say, growing in confidence.

"What?"

"Out in LA, I forgot who I was. Maybe you don't know me, and maybe you never did. Because this is me," I say, gesturing around my room. "Long Sands Beach, the Anderson cottage, the Seabird Motel… those things have made me who I am. So yeah. I guess I did find something pretty damn special when I came back home. I found the real me. I found myself."

"Listen," Victor says calmly. "You don't need to make any

major decisions about us right now. Just know that I do care about you, and I want what's best for you."

His words tug at my heartstrings in every way possible. "I know you want what's best," I say with a sigh. "But maybe the truth is, you don't know what's best for me."

"I do, Summer. I know you better than you think."

"If you know me so well, what am I supposed to do now?"

"Call your agent. Tell them your manager came to get you, and we are going home."

"And then what?"

"Everything goes back to normal. We regroup with the press, we promote your tour, and you crush it. Everything you worked for is yours, and no more cleaning motel rooms. It isn't a good look on you."

CHAPTER THIRTY

It's been two hours since Victor entered Summer's motel room. There are no words to describe how I am feeling in this moment. I am overjoyed with last night and how wonderful Summer was with Kinsley. Seeing them interact together and the joy on my daughter's face was priceless. But the reality of the situation is that Summer and I both have major life decisions to make. There is no doubt in my mind that Victor is in that room, trying to convince her to go home to LA, and part of me wants that for her too. I don't want her to have to give up her career, and there is no way I can turn down Brad's offer. I will be staying in Boston regardless of what Summer decides.

I hear Summer's door open and close, and I peer out my window. Sure enough, Victor is heading down the stairs, toward his car. I realize that she probably needs some time to process whatever it was they talked about. I'm assuming he offered her the life she always wanted on a silver platter. Maybe he was being authentic, and maybe he was telling her what she wanted to hear. I know I should wait for her to reach out to me, but I have this feeling deep within my gut that tells me to go to her. So, I put my pride aside and knock on her door.

"It's me," I say as I knock a couple more times.

Summer comes to the door, wearing my gray sweatshirt over her shorts. Her hair is up in a messy bun, and her eyes are streaked with tears. "Hi," she says, stifling a sob. "You have to stop seeing me like this." She chuckles. "Come in."

I close the door behind me and wrap her in my arms. She rests the side of her face on my chest, and I embrace her close to me. I lose track of how much time has gone by as I hold her, and she cries until finally, she pulls back and looks up at me with thankful eyes.

"It's going to be okay," I say. "We will get through this."

She nods and releases herself from my grip. She flops down on the side of her bed, pulls her knees to her chest, and gestures for me to take a seat next to her. I sit across from her and rub her knee with my palm.

"Well, that sucked," she says with a sigh.

"Is it okay for me to ask what happened? If you don't want to talk about it—"

"No, it's okay." She sniffs. "It's just… it's not going to be easy for you to hear."

My heart sinks as my predictions are confirmed. "I'm tough," I say with a smile. "I can handle it."

"He admitted it. It wasn't my imagination. He has feelings for me, and he's had them for a long time. There was Nova, and then when there wasn't, he just didn't know how to handle it."

"Oh," I say, trying to hide my disappointment. "Do you feel better, knowing that?"

She traces her fingers over mine. "Yes… No… I don't really know. He and Nova broke up. For good."

Now it's my turn to fight the sadness that washes over me. "Wow" is all I can manage to mutter. I stare down at the bedspread, trying to fight off the thoughts that race through my head of all the possible ways this conversation might end.

"There's more. He wants to be with me. He wants to be my manager again. And he wants to clear my name with the press. If I go home tonight, we can sort everything out, and my tour won't be canceled."

Tonight? I think. My heart shatters into a million tiny pieces. My knees grow weak, and I suddenly feel last night's Italian trying to fight its way back up. Her eyes meet mine, and I try with every part of me to stay calm. This girl means the world to me, and even though I want to keep her here with me forever, I know I can't do that. It would be like the time Kinsley trapped a grasshopper in a jar and kept it in her bedroom. She named it Freddy and declared Freddy her pet. I've never seen a human fall in love with an insect like Kinsley loved Freddy. But he lasted a minimum of forty-eight hours before she found him dead, legs up at the bottom of the jar. "What happened to him?" she had asked through tears.

"Grasshoppers don't live in jars," I had tried to explain without making her feel too badly about Freddy's death. "They live out in the wild, and they need to be free."

It is in this moment, as I stare into Summer's eyes and study how conflicted and defeated they are, that I remember Kinsley and her grief. "I just wanted to keep him all to myself," she had wailed. "I wanted to keep him for me, and I killed him." Kinsley grieved Freddy for only a short amount of time, because Sarah and I decided that some sort of pet would be good for our daughter, and Sarah surprised her the next day with a pet canary, who she proceeded to name Freddy.

"What are you thinking?" Summer asks, breaking the silence between us.

I exhale, shake my head, and run my fingers through my hair. How do I find the words to tell her that I think I've found the love of my life in her? How do I tell her that I want to keep her for myself, but that would mean locking her in a jar and suffocating her to death, because she was meant to live wild and free? How do I let her go? Will she even let me? I decide that I need to be strong for her. I will help her make the decision that I know is best for her and her future. Sure, I would love nothing more than for her, Kinsley, and me to be one big happy family, but this is real life, not some fairy tale. If I ask her to stay, it will be a double-edged sword. I have enough experience with relationships—with marriage, even—to know that if I hold her back from her dreams, she will just resent me later. And Victor, Hollywood, her career—those have been her dreams. Not me, River Frost, a divorced single father whose feet are planted on the East Coast, whether he likes it or not. "I think… I think you know what you have to do."

She shakes her head and wipes her tears with her palms. "That's not an answer, River."

"I can't make this decision for you."

"I'm not asking you to make it for me. I just… I want to know what you're thinking about all of this. About us."

"You want me to ask you to stay?" I say, telling her more than asking her.

"Yes. No. I don't know."

"You want me to tell you to go? Go with him?"

"I don't know, River. I don't know what I want."

"I want to be with you, Summer. But I lo—I care about you too much to hold you back. So just tell me. Tell me what you need to hear so that you can choose whatever will make you happy. Because I refuse to be the reason you are held back from your dreams."

Summer throws her arms around me, and I fall back onto

the bed. She climbs on top of me, wrapping her legs around my waist, her sobs increasing rapidly into my neck.

"Tell me what to do, Riv. Please."

"I'm not going to do that," I insist.

"Tell me something, anything, then."

"Summer, I don't know what to say. I honestly feel like this is a lose-lose."

She stares up at me, her hair matted to her tear-streaked face. "Don't ask me to leave," she pleads. "But don't ask me to stay. Just... just leave me somewhere in the middle. Because without you, I'll never be complete."

CHAPTER THIRTY-ONE

Saying goodbye to River was the hardest thing I've ever done. We were lying there together in my bed, just like we had for so many nights prior to today. Only this time, there were only tears. I had begged him for some kind of reason to stay, and he refused to give it to me. I've known him for such a short while, but I know him enough to know that holding me back from LA would be worse than losing me altogether. Why did he have to be so wonderful? This only makes it hurt more.

Victor had flown out this morning, immediately after our conversation, as his flight was out of Logan. After River left my room, demanding I spread my wings and "fly" or something like that and making me promise I would fly back in time to pick up the pieces of my former life, I called my agent, who set me up with a midafternoon flight out of Portsmouth, New Hampshire.

I had thrown all my belongings into my suitcase in less than thirty minutes, packed up my guitar, and said goodbye to Thena. She promised to visit me out in California. Our goodbye was a teary one but not as bad as my farewell conversation with Blake, the one I am having now.

"What happened with River?" he asks, loading my suitcase into the Uber.

"I ended it, I think?" I choke back my tears. "He doesn't want to hold me back. He wants me to go to LA."

"And Victor?"

"What about Victor?"

"Did he apologize?"

"Yes," I said, extending my arms for my hug goodbye.

"So, are you two going to be together?"

"I'm not sure yet. He says he has feelings for me, and he wants a relationship… for real."

Blake nods his head, and since he is still standing there like the moron that he is, I pull him close and hug him goodbye.

"Do you love him?" he asks.

"Victor? I think I've always loved him."

"Why?"

I consider this for a moment. "Do you ever truly know why you love someone?"

"Yeah," Blake says through his laughter. "Typically, you do."

I slide into the Uber and buckle my seat belt. I wave goodbye to my little brother, who has yet to close my door. "Goodbye, Blakey," I say, wiping a tear from my eye. "You were a really great boss," I lie.

But Blake doesn't let me off the hook. "Do you love Riv?"

This question makes me wince. "Blake, I have a flight to catch. Close the door."

"Do you love him?"

I curl my fingers into the sleeves of River's sweatshirt and use them to wipe my tired eyes. "Yes, okay. I love River."

"Why?"

"I don't know, Blake. I just do."

"Why?"

"He gets me, okay? Because at the end of the day, he gets me, Summer Jennings, the little girl from Maine who started talking again because of music, the beach, and her grandmother, Birdie. Because I love this motel more than I love my high-rise out in LA, and River gets that. River would be okay with me cleaning motels for the rest of my life as long it makes me happy."

"Dude. Why are you leaving, then?"

"Because," I sob, trying to pull the door closed. "He doesn't want me to stay. He tells me that he refuses to be the reason I stop performing. And right now, Victor and my career are a freaking package deal, and River knows that, and he's willing to step aside because he is just that awesome, and I suck, and I have to go now, so please just tell your big sister goodbye and that you love her."

Blake kisses me on the cheek and bids me farewell. "Goodbye, big sis. I love you, and I think you're making a mistake."

He closes the door, and I start crying immediately as the Uber pulls out of the parking lot, trying with all my might to catch one last glimpse of River, but he is nowhere to be found. I hold my hand against the window's glass and whisper, "Goodbye."

* * *

IT IS the kind of day that even music can't make better. Voluminous, plump, heavy tears cascade from my tired eyes, splashing in my freshly brewed coffee like raindrops in the ocean. Scratch that. Like raindrops in the ocean during a Category 4 hurricane. Or at least that's how it feels for me.

Have you ever had your heart broken? Have you ever had

so much love for a person, and so much sadness over what could never be, that it overflows out of your eyeballs like a hailstorm? Every. Salty. Drop. Stings. Did you know that airport tears are a different sort of cry? Did you know that just because you love a person with your whole entire being, and even if you would jump in front of a moving freight train for them because you are convinced they are the love of your life, that doesn't mean they will love you back? If you did know this, would you love them anyway?

I cling to my coffee like a lifeline, but even that has lost its usual magic. The bold, rich, flavor that typically warms my soul is overcome with an intrusive tinge of salt thanks to the monsoon that was once my face, but I drink it anyway. I drink it because there is nothing else to do. *Breathe*, I scold. Inhale—the sweetness of my Starbucks Pike Place blend with the uninviting stench of airport. *Exhale. No, really, exhale!* More tears. Sobs. Ugly sobs. Awkward side-eye glances. A tissue. A thank-you that was never successfully spoken into existence.

The memory of his words tugs at my heartstrings. Surely they'll snap at any given moment, like a guitar string wound too tightly or a rubber band stretched too thin. It's just… it's never going to happen, Summer. I'm sorry… it's over.

So let me ask you again. If you survived a broken heart, if you were able to scramble around, picking up the shattered pieces that were once your soul, would you take it all back? Would you erase it all, or would you do it anyway? Love unconditionally, wholeheartedly, like you have nothing to lose even though you really have everything to lose.

I set my coffee cup down on the table beside me and rummage through my bag for my notebook. I locate a pen, overwhelmed with so many emotions I don't even know where to begin. For starters, there is Victor. I was convinced he was the love of my life, and now I'm not too sure about anything. The life he is promising me supercedes anything I could have ever imagined. When I close my eyes, I can picture us together, working together, having fun, loving one another, just being *us*. Victor and I make a great team. We click in all the right ways, and I can't help but wonder how that would transfer romantically, since the one kiss we shared was intoxicating. I mean, I *was* intoxicated, but I'm thinking it would have still been amazing.

Then there is River. Sweet, kind, gentle, mysterious, sexy River. When I'm with him, I feel truly alive. Seeing him with his daughter melts my heart in ways that words just can't describe. I've gotten to know him so well in such a short amount of time, and I love so many things about him. He is genuinely a good listener, and when I tell him about myself, he really cares. When I close my eyes, I can picture us together—him, Kinsley, and me. A family. If this is the case, then how can I walk away from this? How can I get on a plane and fly away from a man that might be the one for me?

I finally put my pen to paper and begin scribbling my thoughts down in fragmented sentences. Some make sense, and some don't, but I don't care. I think back to my motel room this morning and my interactions with both Riv and Victor, and one moment comes to mind. *Don't ask me to leave, but please don't ask me to stay. Leave me somewhere in the middle, because without you, I'll never be complete.* I write this in my notebook and continue writing. My hand can't keep up with the thoughts that swirl through my mind like a tornado. *When you are lonely, count the stars, and I'll count them too. We are both under the same starry sky. You are never truly alone.*

It's like I've opened a can of worms, and every thought and every feeling I have held deep within me over the years pours out of me at lightning speed. *The seagrass is strong because it is not alone. It sticks together, just like us.* A tear lands on the paper, smudging the ink, but I don't stop. *This cottage, this beach, it is who you are. You were made for this. You were made for summer.*

CHAPTER THIRTY-TWO

AUGUST 5, 2023

RIVER FROST

I'm seated at the Sea-Pub and on my third Corona Light when Blake Jennings plops down next to me.

"I'll have what he's having," he says to Ralph. "And he will take another."

"I think," I say, taking a sip of my beer, "that's how this whole mess began."

"Huh?"

"You and I, drinking here at this very bar. You got hammered, I answered Summer's call, and the rest is history."

Blake considers this for a beat, tilts his head, and looks me in the eyes. Like *really* looks me in the eyes. "Do you love her?"

I sip my beer and slam it down on the bar, harder than I intend. "Yeah, man. Of course. I love that woman to death."

Ralph passes a beer to Blake, and he takes a swig. "Then what in the actual hell are you doing sitting here at this bar, feeling sorry for yourself?"

"It's not that simple. You know that."

"I'm not seeing the problem," he argues. "You love her, and she loves you—"

I freeze midsip and turn toward him again. "What did you just say?"

"You love her, and she loves you."

"How do you know that?"

"Know what?"

"That she loves me, you moron."

"Take it easy, dude. She told me. This morning when she was leaving."

"She did?"

"Yeah."

This. Changes. Everything. "Are you sure?"

"Yes, I'm sure," he says, rolling his eyes. "Nobody takes me seriously, ever."

"How could I not know this?"

"Did you ask her?"

"No."

"Well, there you go. No offense, but I think you guys are making this way harder than it needs to be. If you truly love her, ask her to stay."

"I can't do that. She will end up resenting me."

"Why?"

"Her tour, for starters."

"Does she have to live in LA all year to make that happen?"

"Well, no." The guy has a point.

"You could move out there," he suggests.

"No, I can't. I have a daughter, and she lives in Boston with her mother."

"Would they move to LA?"

"Probably not."

"Did you ask them?"

"No."

Blake pats me on the shoulder and swigs his beer once more. "If you asked her to, she would stay."

"What makes you so sure?"

"Because, my man, you were made for this. *You* were made for Summer."

* * *

"Hi!" Oakley squeals. She sits adjacent to me in the back seat of Brad and Thena's SUV.

"Hi!" I say with a wave for what feels like the thousandth time.

"Sorry," Thena says from the passenger seat. "It's her favorite word right now. You can ignore her if you need to."

"I have a daughter," I say with a smile. "I could never do that."

"No you couldn't, could you?" she agrees.

"Hi!" Oakley says again with a wave.

"Hi, Oakley," I say once more.

After Blake's pep talk at the Sea-Pub, I decided to make one last-ditch effort and stop Summer from boarding the plane. After making that decision, I realized I had too much to drink and wouldn't be able to drive myself. Brad and Thena were on their way to the movie set and told me to hop on in. "Five minutes out," I say to nobody in particular.

"What are you going to say?"

"No idea." I chuckle. "But Blake says she loves me. So, I need to try."

"She will be happy to see you, no matter what," Thena says, convinced.

"I sure do hope so."

"Forgive me if I'm being nosy," Brad starts. "But why didn't you ask her to stay?"

"I don't know, man. I can't bring myself to be the one to

hold her back from her life out there. I feel like she will just end up resenting me."

"Did you tell her that?"

"Yes. No… I mean, in a way."

"If I were you, I'd start there. You're a great guy, Riv. One of the things I like about you the most is your honesty and integrity. Just be yourself, and you have nothing to lose."

"Thanks, man. I appreciate it."

We are pulling up to the main entrance to the airport, and my fingers are on the door handle before the car comes to a complete stop.

"Good luck, River," Thena says. "We are rooting for you."

"Thanks so much," I say, unbuckling my seat belt and opening the door.

"Hi!" Oakley says with a wave.

"Hi, Oakley," I say with a smile. I shut the door behind me and begin my mad dash inside the airport, hoping with every ounce of my entire being that I'm not too late.

CHAPTER THIRTY-THREE

AUGUST 5, 2023

SUMMER ROSE JENNINGS

*M*y flight boards in five minutes. I slide my notebook back into my bag, satisfied with my writing. What had started as a simple journal entry just might be my new hit song. I stand to my feet and reach for my guitar case. They strongly suggested I check my guitar with specialty luggage, but I insisted on carrying it on with me until the last possible second. This guitar is a piece of me, and it always will be.

I walk with the flow of traffic toward my gate and notice my flight is on time. I bury my face into the collar of River's sweatshirt and inhale deeply, losing myself in the smell of him but becoming devastated when I realize that there will come a moment when I can't smell his scent anymore. Should I stop smelling it so much? Am I physically removing his smell every time I inhale? My stomach sinks when it hits me that I won't be seeing River tonight. I won't be seeing him tomorrow night or the night after that. I might never see him again. This thought makes my knees wobbly, and I brace myself against the wall for support. What am I doing? Why am I here at this airport instead of back in York with Riv?

"Summer!"

I consider the possibility that I might be losing my mind, because now, not only do I smell River, but I hear him too. I shake my head and close my eyes, begging myself to get it together. But I hear it again, and this time, I know. He's here. River is here at the airport.

"Summer!"

I open my eyes, and there standing before me is a hot and sweaty River Frost. He is out of breath from running, and he is holding a plane ticket in his hand.

"Riv—" I start, but he holds up a hand and stops me midsentence.

"Please. Let me get this out," he says between breaths.

"Okay," I whisper. I drop my guitar case to the ground, and he takes my hands in his.

"I didn't tell you to leave, but I didn't ask you to stay either. I was trying to be fair to you, Summer. I didn't want you to stay because of me because you have such an incredible life out in California, and I couldn't bring myself to keep you from it."

"I—"

"Please," he begs. "Summer Jennings, I love you. I love everything about you. I love that you name songs instead of naming your feelings. I love that you clean motel rooms because it makes you feel close to your grandmother. I love that you have enough self-respect to turn down a loser like Lawson Remington, and I really love that you were humble enough to call me and ask me to help. I love that you wrote notes to me on the Do Not Disturb sign, and I love that you love my hoodies so much. And Summer," he says with a smile, "I really freaking love how you fluff my pillows."

"River, I—"

He holds his hand up to stop me once more. "I don't know what the future looks like for us, Summer, but I know what it doesn't. And it doesn't look like you getting on this plane, at least without me. It doesn't look like the two of us living across the country from each other. It doesn't look like me being with anyone else, and I really hope it doesn't look like you and Victor, because honestly, Summer, I can make you happier than he ever could. Because he will never sit outside the Anderson cottage with you someday while you rock your grandchildren. He will never pride himself on sharing your memories at the Seabird. And I, Summer, I will. I want to take Kinsley to York. I want to stay at the Anderson cottage with her. I want to show her the Nubble Lighthouse. I want to take her to the arcade and win dozens and dozens of tickets with the both of you. I want us to be a family."

"River, please—"

"I'm sorry, Summer. I'm sorry I didn't ask you to stay. But I'm asking you now, baby. Please, please, stay with me. Please don't go. And if you say no, Summer, I'm going to keep asking. I'll ask you over and over again until you say yes, even if it takes one hundred times. But I'll wait," he says, his voice quivering. He holds my face in his hand and steadies my forehead against his. "I'll wait until the hundredth time if that's what you need."

"The hundredth time around?" I ask with a smile. "I see what you did there."

"Ms. Jennings," a flight attendant interrupts, "this is last call. Will you be boarding the plane?"

I laugh at her like she has just made the funniest joke on the planet. "No," I say with certainty. "I won't be boarding the plane."

With that, River picks me up, spins me around, and lets out an overly loud "Yahoo!"

When my feet are steady back on the ground, I stand on my tiptoes and whisper, "Thank you for coming back… and for asking me to stay."

"Come on," he says, kissing me on the top of the head. "Let's get out of here before someone recognizes you. The last thing we need is for them to discover there is a real-life scuba-diving pizza-delivery girl in their airport. The press would be all over it."

"What in the actual—" I start to say, but I stop and simply smile at him. "Hey, Riv?" I say, beaming up at him.

"Yeah?"

"I love you too. Now let's go home."

EPILOGUE

JULY 15, 2024

ONE YEAR LATER

"They are calling for *you!*" Victor exclaims. The smile on his face couldn't be any wider if he tried.

I close my eyes and take it all in. The adrenaline that pumps through my veins is more powerful than any drug, any margarita, or any kiss… Well, maybe not *any* kiss. I have just finished the last song of my first night on tour. The night couldn't have gone any better. Our sold-out venue, the Hollywood Bowl, did not disappoint. It was everything I could have asked for and more.

"Let's go!" Victor cheers, picking me up and spinning me around. "It's encore time. Are you ready?"

"Ready as I'll ever be!" I wrap my arms around Victor's neck and squeeze him tightly. "Thank you," I whisper. "For everything. For all of this."

"You did this, Summer. Don't ever forget it."

"You're the best manager."

"And friend?"

"And friend."

I adjust my battery back in the pocket of my jeans and tuck my hair behind my ear. "I'm going to play it. Acoustic."

Victor nods like he already knew I would choose to debut my newest single during the encore performance. "They are going to love it. They are going to love you."

I jog up the stairs, back onto the stage, and the crowd's cheers wash over me like the biggest waves during the highest of tides. I reach for my guitar and prepare to sing a song that nobody, not even my fiancé, River, has heard yet.

It was my conversation with Birdie that changed everything for me. She and Al had reached out to Blake, overwhelmed with concern, and Blake apparently had spoken to River, per my grandparents' request, and that is how River got the nerve to show up at the airport. Who would have thought Blake and all his annoying-little-brother ways would be the silent hero?

After River and I left the airport in Portsmouth that day, we started brainstorming immediately. There had to be a way that he could keep his job and stay in Boston with Kinsley along with me pursuing my career and not canceling my tour, and we were determined to find the solution. It wasn't until Birdie's postcard reached me at the Seabird Motel that it occurred to me—I *could* have it all. I had instructed Birdie to write me two postcards, one for LA and one for York. That way, I would be guaranteed to receive it. That's when River and I realized that this wasn't an impossible situation at all. I could keep my apartment in LA and live with him in Boston. Sure, there would be a lot of traveling back and forth, but River and Kinsley were worth it, and so was my music.

Confronting Victor was the most difficult factor in the equation. He had made it clear that day in my motel room that he wanted to be with me. He wasn't looking for only a professional relationship. He wanted all of me. He was disappointed to say the least, but in hindsight, we both discovered that he was more interested in Summer Jennings the pop star, not the Summer Jennings I am only now starting to know and love. In the end, Nova and Victor got back together. I was truly happy when I heard this news, and I told them so during my wedding toast.

River and I love our Boston apartment, but it is our time that we spend as a family at the Seabird that makes us the happiest. Kinsley adores York, Maine. She loves the Nubble Lighthouse, Long Sands Beach, and Short Sands Beach. We took her there at the beginning of June, and after surfing at Long Sands and getting ice cream at the Nubble, we met Birdie, Al, and Blake for dinner at the Sea-Pub, where River proposed to me, down on one knee, with the most beautiful diamond ring I have ever seen... stuck to the back of a Do Not Disturb service sign.

Now, as I stand on stage, I'm surrounded by darkness. Darkness and the light that shines from thousands of cell phones held up by fans—my fans. The lights remind me of the stars in the sky, and I fight my desire to count them. I take a deep breath and adjust my mic in its stand and feel like the luckiest girl in the world. "Thank you, everyone, for coming out tonight," I say. More cheers come from the crowd, and I can't fight back my smile. "Tonight is your lucky night," I explain. "I'm going to debut my new single, 'Made for Summer.' You will be the first to hear it!"

I wait a moment for the crowd to settle before playing my first chord. The silence within the venue is eerie. A rush of nervous energy shoots through me, and for a moment, I'm so overcome with emotions that my words stick in the back of my throat, and I'm not able to sing. I turn immediately to the side of the stage, where I know River is positioned with Kinsley. I find his stare, and even through the darkness, the lights, and all of my overwhelming feelings, his eyes calm me down, and I begin to sing:

> You say you might be lonely,
> With no one by your side.
> Shut down all the noises, baby,
> Take a look outside.

> I know it can be scary,
> When you feel you're all alone.
> But count each star one by one,
> And simply come on home.
> Simply come on home.

> I was made for this,
> All my life.
> You were made for me,
> So I'll be your wife.
> You knew who I could be,
> You've watched me become her.
> You were made for me,
> You were made for Summer.

I RUSH OFF STAGE, and this time, I run toward Kinsley, who is already leaping midair into my arms.

"I'm proud of you," she whispers in my ear.

"You liked it?"

"I loved it, Summer."

"Maybe next time, you can sing it with me?"

"Yes!" she shrieks, and I squeeze her again.

River takes Kinsley from me and places her back down on the ground, but she doesn't let go of my hand. I steady my gaze on his and search his eyes for evidence that he liked the song. I can tell he does, but I ask anyway. "Did you like it?"

River traces the side of my face with his index finger and wipes a tear from my eye. "You know I loved it."

"I wrote it for you, you know."

"Yeah," he says, wiping a tear from his own eye. "I figured that was about me."

"I thought maybe that could be our wedding song," I say with a wink.

"I was thinking the same thing," he says, pulling me close and kissing me like we are the only two people on earth.

When he pulls back, he smiles and says, "Come on. Let's go home."

"But we are *very* far from home," Kinsley says.

"Nah," I say to her with a smile. "Did you know that people can feel like home? As long as we have each other, Kinsley, we will always be home."

SUMMER'S PLAYLIST 🎵

AVAILABLE ON SPOTIFY

- Guns N' Roses, 'November Rain'
- The Flamingos, 'I Only Have Eyes for You'
- Dave Matthew's, 'Satellite'
- Dan & Shay, 'Tequila'
- Bishop Briggs, 'River'
- Adel, 'Make You Feel My Love'
- Hinder, 'Lips of an Angel'
- Alicia Keys, 'This Girl is on Fire'
- Luke Bryan, 'One Margarita'
- Three Doors Down, 'Here Without You'
- Lifehouse, 'Somewhere in Between'
- Snow Patrol, 'Chasing Cars'
- Charlie Puth, 'One Call Away'
- Bryan Adams, 'Let's Make a Night to Remember'
- Third Eye Blind, 'How's it gonna be?'

* Summer Jennings, 'When I'm With You'
* Summer Jennings, 'Made for Summer'

STAY TUNED...

THE GENERATION BEACH SERIES BY:
STACY LEE

All good things must come to an end, but the memories created on Long Sands Beach last for generations.

Be on the lookout for the Generation Beach Series, a spinoff of the Nubble Light Series, where young characters have grown, older characters remain young at heart, and the magic of the East Coast remains majestically spectacular.

OPERATION SUPERGLUE BY: STACY LEE

A little glue goes a long way.

Or at least that's what thirty-five-year- old single mother, Lina Rivera hopes for when she finds herself smack dab in the middle of an undercover operation as a high school senior.

Best-selling young adult crime novelist, Lina Rivera is strikingly beautiful and can't even purchase a scratch ticket without being carded. With her twins Luciana and Max beginning their freshman year of high school in the fall, she has never felt closer to understanding her target demographic—teenagers. But when the reviews for her newest release fall short, and negative feedback taunts her from every angle, it becomes clear that teenage life in 2024 is nothing like her high experience back in 1999...and people are starting to notice.

Against popular opinion, Lina is desperate to continue writing young adult books. So, when her ex-husband and private investigator Jon Cote invites her on board an undercover operation at a local private high school, she *can't* say no. In effort to target reasons why multiple female students have run away from home, Jon has discovered a more seriously dangerous pattern...so much so he finds himself leading Operation Superglue, posing as the school's art substitute.

Now, an undercover high school senior, Lina learns that today's society is worlds away from familiar. And with her ex-husband back in her life in more ways than one, Lina learns quickly that choices she's made in the past just might not have to be as permanently sticky as she once assumed they would be.

ABOUT THE AUTHOR

Stacy Lee is the author of the Nubble Light Series. Stacy is a lifelong resident of New England. She lives in New Hampshire with her incredibly supportive husband, two beautiful children, and two well loved (spoiled) rescue pups. She enjoys spending time in the beautiful and historic town of York Beach, Maine with her family. The Nubble Lighthouse holds a special place in her heart.

Before she started writing women's fiction, Stacy received her bachelor's degree in elementary education with a teacher certification in grades K-8. She taught elementary school and writing courses to students for fourteen years while completing a graduate degree in elementary administration where she graduated with honors. After that, (in an effort to drive her husband completely crazy) decided to switch careers and go to Bible College, where she graduated with a Master's in Christian Ministry with a focus in Homiletics. Finally, when she got tired of taking college courses she decided to pursue her dream as an author. She is thankful for her husband and his ability to bring out the best in her...always.

ALSO BY STACY LEE

The Hundredth Time Around- Book one of the Nubble Light
Series

Future Plans- Book two of the Nubble Light Series

Never in a Billion- Book three of the Nubble Light Series

Ten Percent of my Heart-Book four of the Nubble Light Series